The Secret Li
an Anthol
Longish-Sho
by Lizzie Jarrett

Copyright © 2019 by the author known in the UK as Lizzie Jarrett, details upon application.

All rights reserved. This book or any portion thereof may not be reproduced or used in any manner whatsoever without the express written permission of the author, except for the use of brief quotations in a book review.

Printed in the United Kingdom
First Printing:2022
ISBN: 9798843866723

Contents	Page
The Secret Life of Trees	5
My Father's Suitcase	39
The Cutting Room Floor	61
Demonic	85
The Friendly Society of Witches	101
The Ring of Unluck	125
Lunex Insurance Services	149
The Way Forward?	177

Special thanks to Marion Wilmot and Will Heap for their kind words of encouragement.

of a forest, because there have been complaints of a certain type of "undesirable activity" in the Golf Club car park. Needing to take a leak he had stumbled through the undergrowth to find some privacy. Turning to go back to his unmarked car in the car park he heard the sound of a tiny yawn behind him. There she lay at the foot of the tree; tiny, naked and unprotected.

5. Authority figures

Sergeant Pete radios back to headquarters.
'What did he say?' says Sharon Oliver, one of the call handlers.
'He said a naked three year old child, it must be something to do with those weirdos at the Golf Club car park. Honestly some people!' James Bennett raises his eyes heavenwards and phones the Social Work team to suggest they get down to the Golf Club as soon as possible.

By the time that Sergeant Pete and the social worker arrive back at the police station, the tiny girl is swathed in a big blue blanket into which she now sinks, to take cover from the many curious pairs of eyes that now seem to bore into her.

'Well, you know Pete, I'd love to have her, but Mum wouldn't like it and you know what she's like. One mention of darker skin and she'll be off on one...'
Sergeant Pete sighs. Quite often the words "Wouldn't it be great to live as one big happy

family?" came back to haunt him. His mother-in-law is the reason he no longer wishes to return home at the end of his very long shifts. There she will be in the kitchen, cooking up some foul concoction from the culinary years that time forgot and raising her eyes heavenwards, as he steps through his own front door.

He wants to go home, his bed is calling to him, but he has a tiny charge to take care of first. On the phone to his fifth children's home of the night, he is desperate to find the little girl a place of safety.

'Will you take her then? She's only tiny. No, we don't know who she is or where she comes from, so it's probably going to be a long-term fostering or possibly adoption'.

Sergeant Pete finds himself driving at 3am to a children's home north of the town.
'Le Petit Manoir, what kind of a name is that?' Pete finds himself asking this question out loud, but then he is very tired now and he needs to get home to his bed.

6. Le Petit Manoir

Le Petit Manoir children's home is under the flight path of the nearby airport, every 15 minutes the very foundations of the building shake and reverberate as engines kick into action and aeroplanes belt along the runway and up into the sky. The passengers onboard the 747s and DC10s

The Secret Life of Trees: an Anthology of Longish-Short Stories
by Lizzie Jarrett

The Secret Life of Trees

1. Awakening

The beech tree heaved and shuddered along all of its branches and its leaves shimmered in ecstasy. The roots lifted and sank, as this huge giant seemed to rock back and forth. Eventually and with a huge moan, which seemed to come from its very heart, the trunk itself split open. Out of this wound there stepped a tiny and perfect child.

The forest seemed to enter a becalmed state, as though it were denying what it had just witnessed. The wind dropped and the trees stood perfectly still; playing a game of giant woodland statues. The birds perched motionless in their nests, daring each other to make the first move. Squirrels stood pinned to the sides of the last tree they had been playing on, flexing their furry leg muscles like nervous sprinters ready for the starting gun. Everything and everyone was in a state of suppressed anticipation.

The tiny, perfect girl child looked up in awe at her surroundings. Then she strolled purposefully out from the cover of the trees, as if she were about to take a pleasant morning walk.

Standing about three feet tall, her skin was decidedly sallow, her long brown hair hung down around her like a modesty veil. Behind the veil of hair a pair of huge green eyes flicked nervously back and forth.

The mother tree itself groaned again and as sap gushed from the trunk, the forest seemed to burst into life again like a round of applause. The wind picked up and the leaves in the trees rippled as if they were flags on bunting. The bird life piped up like a woodland marching band and the squirrels resumed their endless pursuit of food, as they rattled up and down the branches of the trees.

2. The Perfect Wife

'Mummy, mummy can we take this little girl home with us?' little Timmy Snow has been playing contentedly all afternoon with his new friend whom he found in the forest, now he wants to take her home.

Susan Snow, the perfect wife, keeper of the immaculate home, is not going to countenance such a suggestion. She has her life organised pretty perfectly, thank you very much, and taking care of another child does not fit into her plan, and that includes imaginary friends.

'But Mummy she's real...' protests Timmy, as he stares in vain out of the back window of the Range Rover. Timmy looks in disgust at their pet poodle, Sasha.
'Stupid dog.' thinks Timmy, 'I'd much rather have a sister..'.

Susan Snow has decided that *that* is never going to happen.

3. Nightfall

The little girl began to tire after her first, long and eventful day on earth. Firstly, she had arrived fully-formed in the middle of the forest and then she had found a friend for the afternoon; in the form of Timmy Snow. Whether Timmy's mother believed it or not, he really had found a genuine friend for the afternoon.

The tiny little thing rubbed her eyes and stumbled back to the mother tree, where the wound had first opened…it had now sealed shut and in its place was a newly-formed scar. The tree now seemed remote and unaware of her existence. The tiny child snuggled herself down at the roots, draped her long hair around her and went to sleep.

4. Discovery

'Well, what have we got here?'
Two big brown eyes looked down into the little girl's big green eyes. Sergeant Pete Woods is a big-hearted guy, but in all his thirty years on the force he's never seen anything like this.

Snuggled up into a perfect cocoon of her own hair is a tiny, naked girl. Sergeant Pete feels as if he is an extra in a film of The Jungle Book. He is only patrolling this late at night, on his own at the edge are making their escape to pastures new, the occupants of Le Petit Manoir are simply planning their escape.

'Look at her. What's she wearing?'
'Where did she come from?'
'She just turned up overnight'.
Our tiny little heroine has opened those big green eyes this morning to find herself looking back into more eyes than she can comprehend.

In their hurry to find something for their tiny midnight visitor to wear, the duty officer had phoned his wife who was still on duty at the local 24 hour supermarket. There had been a major miscommunication and for some reason she had brought along a Sleeping Beauty fancy dress costume for a three year old.

This tiny Disney princess is sitting up now, maybe she should have been dressed as Rapunzel; since her hair has spread out like a magic cloak and it is dangling down over the sides of the bed. She can see now what, or who, is looking at her. They are a ragtag assortment of children of different ages and sizes ranging from a snotty nosed five year old to a tall sulky girl of seventeen or so.

Children's homes and short-term fostering in the Surrey area"

"Set in an idyllic countryside setting Le Petit Manoir children's home is housed in a large 7 bedroom house originally built in the 1930s. This home currently houses 8 children, with room for emergency cases if necessary. All ages catered for. Children over the age of 5 will be provided with a mini-bus to local state schools in the area. The current management will not cater for behavioural issues...."

There they sat in front of her; the unloved, the unwanted and the unknown. The sulky 17 year old girl turned out to be Michelle Noakes, father from the West Indies, mother from "God-knows-where", Surrey. The snotty child was Kevin Vowels, His blonde hair was cut in an awkward bowl cut and it stuck out in a static halo around his head. He had a cold 365 days of the year and his nose ran constantly. His sister, Denise, who was only 10 was always just a minute too late presenting Kevin with a hanky, which she carried concealed up her sleeve. Denise was both sister and mother to the unappealing little tot, whom she adored nonetheless.

The twins, Derek and Michael Jones, were as closely joined as their thick National Health frames were sellotaped together with great ugly reams of tape. Miss Maitland would frequently claim money from the county for the twins to have new glasses, but somehow or another they never got their nice new frames. The lady of the "manoir", however, always had extra money in the kitty to buy another ghastly chiffon scarf or perhaps something nasty and alcoholic for the drinks cabinet.

Shelley Adams and Julie Martin, both aged 13, clung together for friendship and reinforcement of a sense of self. It was a delicate balance of love and mutual tolerance, bordering on loathing and jealousy. Introduce one more 13 year old girl and that delicate balance would be pushed into the danger zone.

Last of all was Ian Holland, his only wish was to be left alone and most of the time the other children could manage this. Ian's chief interest was computing. There was a Computer club at school, which Ian was allowed to stay late for, but Le Petit Manoir would not stretch to a computer; so he would read his computer magazines alone and he would sketch designs for computers, but to talk to anyone would be sheer torture.

7. An Unexpected Turn of Events

"*Instructions:*
  1. *Remove the plastic cap to expose the absorbent window.*
  2. *Point the absorbent tip (marked with the green arrow) directly into the urine stream. Take the sample for at least 10 seconds, to ensure that an adequate sample is collected.*
  3. *Replace the cap and place it horizontally on a clean, flat surface. Wait 5 minutes for the test to finish processing.*"

Someone else is waking up to a new horizon today. As Susan Snow swings her feet out of bed and into her quilted nylon slippers she feels a sudden familiar feeling in the back of her throat. An awful retching sickness, just like four years ago when she was ….'Oh my God, I can't be pregnant…no, no that will ruin everything'. Timmy, on the other hand, can look forward to having a little playmate of his own.

8. The Great Escape

"Avenir Cruises

Steal away to one of our exotic locations, leave all your worries behind as you embark on a new adventure with Avenir Cruises.

Choose from one of our three destination packages and make all your dreams come true.

The Caribbean

Fantastic Espana

The Ancient World: Italy and Greece.

Tel: Newbridge: 79733 and ask for more details."

It has long been a cherished dream of Annie Woods to visit Greece or Italy, but both in one holiday surpasses all her expectations. However, at 53 she still finds herself sheltering in the bathroom reading a holiday catalogue that seems heaven sent. The one thing standing in the way of her achieving this dream is her mother, the redoubtable Mrs. Elsie Gathercole.

Annie is Elsie's only child still left on this side of the Atlantic or Pacific Oceans. Her brother, Ray and younger sister, Pat, had left this country as soon as they could get together the money for a one way ticket. In some ways she had to take her hat off to them, what were they mind-readers? Annie had made her mother a promise at the age of 6 to look after her as long as she lived. She believed that if you were kind to people they would be kind to you in return.

In her husband she had found a kind and loving partner who was patience itself. Nothing was ever too much trouble for Sergeant Pete Woods, just look at the way he had looked after that poor little waif the other night. However, little did Annie and Pete know that when they had opened up their home to Annie's mother that their lives would never be the same again.

Every move was watched, every decision questioned, every sore opened. Whilst Pete, at least, had the sanctuary of his job, Annie had always intended to get a little job after the children had grown up, but infertility had put paid to that plan and whilst it was true that Pete and Annie had no children, they surely did have one big baby. Unfortunately it was seventy-five years old and was standing, not too patiently, on the other side of the bathroom door.

'What are you doing in there? How long are you going to be? I need to spend a penny, so hurry up young lady!' Elsie rattled on from the hallway.

Holiday brochure in hand, Annie exited the bathroom and tried to walk at top speed towards the kitchen, before being apprehended.

'What have you got there?...Holiday cruises, you can't afford those and anyway what am I going to do if you away? You never thought about that, did you?' Elsie continued on her tirade.
'It can't hurt to look though, can it Mum? I am sure Pete would love to go on a cruise.'

Annie felt quite aggrieved, she'd been putting off a big holiday for years. She and Pete had saved up quite a sizeable sum, easily enough to pay for a cruise holiday; now a certain somebody was threatening to take it all away.

During this exchange Sergeant Pete had emerged from the master bedroom upstairs. He wanted to stroll out to the back garden to look at his tulips, the only problem was that he had to go straight through the kitchen to get there.
'What do you think Pete, it would be lovely, wouldn't it? A cruise to both Italy and Greece?' said his wife plaintively, as Pete tried to turn the back door key to escape outside. In all honesty

Sergeant Pete was happy wherever he went, as long as it was just him and Annie, but now it *never* was just him and Annie, it was *always* the uncomfortable three's a crowd; Pete and Annie and Elsie.
'You go ahead and give them a call love, if that's what you want' that was Pete's parting shot as he ran for the sanctuary of the garden.

Pete loved his garden with its carefully tended green square of perfectly level grass, his shed at the end of the garden and the patio; where last weekend he had placed two tubs of tulips. He breathed in the fresh spring air and let his shoulders relax, as he sauntered round his own little kingdom.

Through the double glazing he could see his wife and mother-in-law continue their "discussion", since they had now moved to the lounge. Pete liked to imagine exactly what his mother-in-law was saying. He could almost write a script for her. "Who do you think you are young lady?" was one of her all-time top ten hits along with "I never want to go abroad, it's all full of coloureds." Pete looked through the glass again, but he simply saw his wife peering back at him and gesturing furiously. What was she saying? 'Get a ….? Get a ….?' Now she was miming something with her fingers, she was using her index finger in a clockwise manner, as if she were dialling a number on a telephone. He looked round the side of this agitated dumbshow to see his mother-in-law lying motionless on the floor. By the time he had raced back into the house he could see that it was already too late for an ambulance.

9. Lady of the "Manoir"

Back at Le Petit Manoir the latest addition to the ranks suddenly became aware of a presence in the room, it is a malign presence. Eliza Maitland, lady of the "manoir"; that is definitely how she sees herself and the children are her serfs and vassals.

She had always been taller than everyone else in the room, she stood at a good 6' 2". When she had been a child this had worked to her disadvantage because adults always assumed she was at least 5 years older than she actually was. Children of her own age, on the other hand, were always frightened of her and never wanted to be friends. Blessed as she was with a very long and prominent nose and horse-like teeth, she found it hard to fade into the background of any room. She still struggled to forgive children-kind as a whole for deserting and alienating her in her own childhood and she carried her grudge around with her in her daily life. Never had someone been so ill-suited to work in child care.

'Good morning everybody, I see you've all met "Teresa Green", our little visitor from the forest. So now you've all said your "Hellos" you had better get on with your chores,' and with that her troops were dismissed for the day.

Miss Maitland is extremely pleased with her stroke of genius at naming the little girl "Teresa". She found it extremely amusing at whatever o'clock in the morning to be "christening" the child with what she thought was an amusing name. It had taken her all of two seconds to dream the name up, she didn't care whether or not it might be the source of derision for years to come.

The children's chores were as follows: Michelle, childcare; she would be Teresa's day-to-day carer. Kevin and Denise, food preparation, Derek and Michael, gardening chores and any other external jobs. Shelley and Julie, household cleaning and Ian, anything electrical and indoor DIY.

Miss Maitland's logic was that the more the children were kept active, the less she would have to look at them. The less those tiny childish eyes could stare back into her large over-made up eyes, laden with mascara. Those eyes that questioned her; "Why are you doing this? What have we ever done to you?"

Miss Maitland is extremely annoyed that she has been lumbered with a three year old, what use has she for someone that won't and can't work? Better to lock Michelle and Teresa upstairs where she can't see them, keep them out of the way. So it is from this vantage point on Teresa's first full day that she and Michelle can see the twins walking around the large and overgrown garden with a very rusty set of gardening tools trying to tidy the place up.

Today they have been tasked with hacking down a holly bush that had got out of control and was smothering the tree underneath. The holly had grown up around the original tree, hiding its identity. It formed a spiky fence around other weaker trees blocking out the light; nothing could thrive underneath, apart from stunted and misshapen fungi and weirdly pale slugs and maggots in under-developed tones.

Derek and Michael appeared at the base of the tree like two little Munchkins trying to duel with a superior opponent. Every time they made another foray within the reach of the holly they emerged scarred and bloodied. Derek came to the back door to ask for a plaster for Michael, but was sent back into battle by Miss Maitland and told to "Stop fussing!".

When at last the bulk of the holly lay on the grass it was time for the boys to cut down a beech tree that stood in the corner of the garden. Miss Maitland required the tree for firewood. They worked as a team taking turns to hack their rusty axes into the trunk of the tree. For a team of ten year olds it was admirable work. Just as the tree was starting to lean to one side Michael turned towards the house; as if seeking some kind of approval. As he stood there smiling at his brother, with the sun glinting on the thick lenses of his glasses, there was a sickening creak and then a dull thud as the full weight of the tree landed on him.

10: Bluebell Ward

"Built in 1965 to accommodate expanding demand, Newtown hospital is a 300 bed facility in the centre of the town. There is a male surgical ward, a female surgical ward, a geriatric ward and a children's ward. Visiting hours are from 2pm onward, please try not to overtire the patients, they are here to get better......

Bluebell Ward is for children aged 3 to 14. A vibrant colour scheme and cheery murals of cartoon characters aim to keep our young patients calm, happy and relaxed during their time in hospital.

Newtown General Hospital; a guide for visitors."

There was a smell of disinfectant and a persistent 'beep, beep, beep' noise, strange and unfamiliar ceiling tiles stretched away overhead. The bed in which he was lying was frighteningly clean and had starched cotton sheets. Michael knew he was not at Le Petit Manoir anymore.

'Hallo Michael and how are you today?', enquired a friendly voice. Michael looked up, he could see a nice smiling West Indian lady wearing a white apron and with her watch on upside down. Michael is in the Bluebell ward at the local hospital. He's had a very close shave, the weight of the tree fell across his leg causing a clean break and a big enough shock to make him pass out. Had the tree fallen six inches to the left Michael would never have woken up again. The lovely smiling nurse offers him a nice drink of sugary squash and then she returns to her other patients. Michael thinks she is the most beautiful thing he has ever seen.

11. Bloody do-gooders

Ever since Michael's stay in hospital, Miss Maitland has had several extra phone calls from Social Services. This evening they wanted to know a number of things about Derek and Michael. How had they managed to break into the tool shed? Where were the keys for the shed kept? Was this kind of rebellious behaviour frequently observed? Had other children been involved? There was even talk of an upcoming inspection.

Miss Maitland pushed the end of the cigarette she was smoking into the glass ashtray next to the phone, as she slammed the phone back into its holster. She then exclaimed loudly enough for everyone to hear. 'Bloody kids, bloody Social Services busy-bodies, bloody do-gooders!'

She looked out into the garden, just to the left of the fallen tree. Where there had been nothing before, there was now a large overgrown weed. It had sprung up to over 9 feet in height, with shapeless, unattractive, oversized leaves, but it was a weed nonetheless.

12. In Denial

"Dictated to Mrs. A. Lee
From: Mr. J. Trivett
To: Dr. P. Wordsworth, GP

Dear Peter

re: Mrs. S. Snow.
b.11.1.1965

I saw this lady today, she is at the 16 week stage of pregnancy, she is convinced there has been a mistake of some description. Throughout my examination of her she continued to assert that she had not had marital relations with her husband for some two years and that it was therefore impossible that she be pregnant.

In short, my examination of her confirmed that she is indeed with child. I have advised her to come to terms with the forthcoming event. Should she visit you I would like to kindly advise you against prescribing anti-depressants or sedatives of any kind.

It is my firm medical opinion that this is a healthy pregnancy and therefore should not be compromised in any way.

With very best wishes

Josh

Mr. J. Trivett

Susan sends her best wishes to yourself, Barbara, and the family"

13. Evening visitors

Kevin and Denise are cooking dinner tonight, they are making Shepherd's Pie. Kevin has already peeled a big bucket of potatoes and put them onto boil.
'I've done the 'taters' sis'. He sniffs loudly and then blows his nose.
'Well done Kev' says Denise proudly, patting him on the back.
Miss Maitland has told them to have dinner ready extra early because she is expecting visitors. Kevin sniffs again, and wipes his nose on his sleeve, whilst Denise start frying up the mince.

Once dinner has been served, eaten and washed up, all of the children are sent up to their rooms for the evening. There is a ring on the doorbell and the children can then hear voices downstairs. After about 30 minutes Shelley and Julie can hear someone tapping on their bedroom door. It is Miss Maitland; she is smiling in what can only be called an uncharacteristic manner. It is quite alarming…

In the front lounge sit four men. Shelley and Julie have never seen them before. Miss Maitland simply appeared outside their bedroom door and told them to put on their best clothes and make-up and come downstairs. Shelley doesn't like the men, they are really old and one of them keeps laughing and trying to give her a cuddle.

14. Out of sight, out of mind

Back in their bedrooms the other children sit listening to the sound of laughter coming from behind the closed and locked doors. Kevin gets tired after a while and falls asleep with his thumb wedged firmly in his mouth.

Ian thinks nothing of it, this is routine for him; being isolated and alone. Mentally he plans ahead, anything must be better than this he thinks.

Michelle puts little Teresa to bed. For all her sulkiness and her teenage years she already feels quite attached towards the little girl and is trying to do her best to look after her.

Derek hardly ever comes downstairs nowadays and has been lying in bed since midday. Only Denise feels cheated, she heard Miss Maitland come and fetch Shelley and Julie from their room and she feels jealous that she was not selected too.

Downstairs a rather predictable scenario is playing out, two rather tipsy teenage girls are sitting on the sofas alongside their evening visitors. They are feeling by turns excited and frightened by what is going on. They get to stay up late, wear make-up and get to drink Babycham and Gin and Orange; what could possibly be the downside to this arrangement?

Miss Maitland watches with proprietorial pride as this scenario plays out in front of her. Had the woman no shame? It is only later as she climbs up the stairs to bed that she shivers inwardly. She feels as if she is being watched, but by what, or by whom, she couldn't tell you.

Outside in the garden the trunk of the huge weed, that had now taken pride of place in the garden, seemed to thicken like a deformed black tumour. Its spindly branches became covered in slippery blackened moss. Whilst at the roots tiny fungal spores erupted and the grass around the tree started to wither and die.

15. Mrs. Graham

"Hospital visitor scheme:

Do you have what it takes to visit a needy child in hospital? Some of our patients are orphans or cared for children and do not receive family visits. Initial research has shown that receiving regular visits contributes to a faster recovery and a shorter overall hospital stay.

If you think you can spare two hours a week to make the difference, please ring this number and ask for Angela.
Newtown 34549"

Little Michael Jones is flourishing in hospital, the lovely nurse watches over him at night and sometimes, during the day, a really kind lady called Mrs. Graham comes to visit. She brings him sweets, which the nurse allows him to have, and next week Mrs. Graham says she will bring him a Snoopy cuddly toy. Michael has always wanted a toy for himself, anything that hadn't passed through hundreds of grubby hands before it got to him.

Derek, on the other hand, is wilting away; deprived of Michael's company he has become tired and listless. He doesn't know how to operate without his twin.

16. Holiday Dreams

Thousands of miles away and standing on the prow of the MV. Holiday Dreams are a contented middle-aged couple; in love with each other and in love with the moment. They have already been enchanted with Italy and visited sites of historical interest there, now they are their way to Greece.

For Annie Woods this is the crowning moment of a long cherished dream, she looks lovingly at her husband and drinks in the moment. Their life is *almost* perfect; the only thing missing is a child. Annie knows that Pete feels the void as keenly as she does, but knows in her heart it is really too late to do anything about it. She sighs deeply and turns to look at her husband again, who, unbeknownst to her, is wondering whatever happened to the tiny child who he found in the forest all those months ago.

17. Everyday nightmare

Does the world divide into two kinds of people? There are those that are just out there for themselves and those that seek to help others. There are those that seek solely to take and have no use for loving comfort, whilst others need to give and receive love. These were questions that never troubled Miss Eliza Maitland, of course she was there to help herself, who else would you help? She had been put in this position of power not to help or love the children, but to make them realise that life was difficult and hard and that no-one owed you anything. Nobody would ever do anything for you out of love, if you believed that you were a fool.

In Miss Maitland's mind there were two types of people; those that she could find a use for and those that she couldn't. At the moment, Shelley and Julie were useful to her and so were Kevin and Denise, but what possible use were the others? Ian, the social outcast, Derek, short-sighted, pale and ill and as for that half-caste girl and the baby, what use were they?

18. The Handsome Stranger

Luckily Miss Maitland doesn't run the world, she can control Le Petit Manoir, but she can't control what goes on in the garden next door. For this very evening there appears on the lawn next door, an image of masculine beauty. He is tall, he is raven-haired, he is well-muscled and he has decided to play football. It is as if he were made to order from Michelle's teenage dreams.

First, he does 100 "keepie-uppies", showing to good advantage his bulging thigh muscles as he does so. Then he dribbles the ball back and forth across the lawn, so that Michelle can see his fine form, both from the front and from behind. Finally, as if to seal the deal, he kicks the ball repeatedly into the goal at the far end of the garden, displaying his sheer masculine strength and virility.

Michelle looks on admiringly with her heart pounding. She turns round guiltily, but sees little Teresa is simply sleeping peacefully with a serene and almost meditative look on her face. If Michelle had been able to glance back quickly, she would have seen her football hero gazing up at the window with a determined look upon his handsome face.

19. One for the journals

"To: Dr. J. Cowley
Professor of Dermatology
Kings College Hospital
Denmark Hill
London

Dear John

I thought this case might be of interest to you, interested as you are in all dermatological peculiarities. A female patient has presented with the most unusual symptoms. The patient is extremely tall, about 6' 2", she has been attempting to treat her afflictions herself, with no success. Her symptoms are as follows: a "moss-like" substance appearing on her underarms and calves, an outcrop of small fungal spores erupting from the top of both feet. To crown it all this unfortunate, and I am afraid to say unpleasant, woman also complains that her hair growth is now extremely coarse and is almost "twig-like".

If you have any insight as to the possible prognosis for this patient and/or any known treatment, please ring my secretary, Norma. This might be one for the journals!

Best Wishes

Jonty Wilkes

Dr. J. Wilkes
Newtown General Hospital"

Upstairs in her bedroom at Le Petit Manoir, a tall and rather unpleasant woman is hiding underneath her candlewick covers. She has had another nightmare, a bad dream in which she is pursued everywhere by a huge pair of green eyes. She struggles out of bed and stares into the mirror, she half expects to see those big green eyes staring back at her. But the only thing she can see is her twisted, distorted reflection. Her face has grown so contorted and furrowed recently. There is only so much that make-up can cover; she doesn't know what to do with herself. The phone is ringing again downstairs. She bolts back to her bed, pulls the pillow up over her coarsened, hardened hair and blocks out the noise.

20. Snoopy

Michael is sitting up in bed today and cuddling his Snoopy toy with all his might, Mrs. Graham and her husband have both arrived today and are in earnest conversation with the ward sister. Michael can overhear the occasional snippet.
'Yes, yes, terrible woman'
'…he has a twin…?'
Michael hugs Snoopy intently while trying to look as though he isn't listening in. The lovely nurse and Mr. and Mrs. Graham are now heading over towards his bed.
'Well Michael, you're so much better, it will soon be time to go back home.' said the nurse, in an unstudied tone.
'No, no, I need to stay here, I don't feel very good.' says Michael
'What if you could go home with Mr. and Mrs. Graham instead?' says the nurse wistfully.

21. Sean

'Thwock!' There is a noise coming from outside. 'Thwock!' there it goes again. Michelle tiptoes out of bed and edges towards the window, as she pulls back the curtain, she sees what is making the noise.

A flying clump of dried clay has just hit the window and down below, standing in the middle of the long grass in the garden, is the footballer from next door. He is gesturing at her to open the window. She does so.

'Hi there gorgeous' shouts the late night visitor 'I'm Sean. I live next door. What's your name?'
Thrilled, but frightened at the same time, Michelle leans out of the window and places her finger across her lips. 'Ssh, she'll hear you. I'm Michelle, I'm locked into my bedroom and so is everyone else.'
'Bloody hell! What's going on in there?' exclaims her Prince Charming.

Before the conversation can get any further, through the door erupts the most frightening vision. It is Miss Maitland, but she looks deformed. Her hair sticks out like an unruly bird's nest, her face is blotchy and diseased and her stomach bulges out strangely; she is in no mood to be argued with. With one clumsy and graceless move she pulls the window shut and follows through to knock Michelle to the floor.

'Don't get ideas above your station, you ugly girl!' screams the demented vision.

As she pulls her huge shapeless dressing gown around her strange and deformed body, her eyes fall on the little child cowering behind Michelle.

Through the brown curtain of the child's hair peer a pair of luminous green eyes.

'Don't you stare at me you little freak. I'll show you who's in charge here!' screams the unholy witch, as she raises her hand to hit the child. But even as the words exit her mouth, her arm will not comply with its owner's wish and it remains raised above her head unable to complete its downward path. Incapacitated by rage she runs screaming from the room, hand still held aloft.

Michelle pulled herself up onto her knees and looked round towards the child, who was now staring in concentrated rage and fury at the open door.

'What is going on in your mind Teresa?' Michelle says, and then with an after-thought she adds 'life's not meant to be like this, you know'.

22. The Perfect Family

'Breathe, breathe, breathe....there's a good girl! You're almost there, I can see the head. Now I'm going to need you to give one more big push' says the midwife to her patient.

'I can't, I can't manage it...please give me some more gas and air' says the mother to be. The mother takes a big lungful of the Entonox and looks very, very relaxed. She is so completely relaxed she has now gone to sleep.

'Wake up Susan, you've still got a job to do. Come on then Susan, one big push…you can do it'

Looking up through the sleepy haze, Susan Snow sees her husband, Richard, smiling lovingly at her.
'Come on Susie, you can do it' he says.
Susan can't remember the last time he called her Susie, come to that the whole of the last nine months has been very confusing, how could she actually be pregnant, how could she be giving birth right NOW?
'OW! OW! THAT HURTS, THAT REALLY, REALLY HURTS!'

Suddenly there is silence and then a small cry. Before she fully realises that the pain is now all over, she is presented with a tiny pink bundle, wrapped in a pink babygro.

'Oh, she's so-o beautiful! What shall we call her?' says Susan.
'Why don't we ask Timmy? I think he would like to have the final say. After all he has always wanted a sister.' replies her husband.

23.

"THE DAILY VOICE

Sex Abuse and Child Labour at "Le Petit Manoir"

Read inside for shocking details of abuse at yet another children's home.

"They locked us in our rooms!"
Underage girls forced to act as hostesses at seedy drinks parties.
"We thought that these men were there to help us….!"
A number of hitherto respected local businessmen are helping police with their enquiries……

The chief offender, Eliza Maitland, somehow managed to evade police custody. Anyone knowing of her whereabouts should contact Surrey Police immediately. It is understood she may have taken a child as a prisoner. A young child known as "Teresa Green" has not been seen since the evening of the 21st of June……

Our main informant, who wishes to remain anonymous, had made use of his impressive knowledge of computers and cameras to rig up a surveillance system that has recorded various incidents. These included offences under the Employment of Minors Act and countless offences regarding the Sexual Exploitation of Minors, in addition to these offences there was a frequent and flagrant disregard for health and safety regulations.

Chief Reporter: Alyson Brinsden"

24. Good neighbours

Sean O'Herlihy, centre-half for Newtown Wanderers, always tells his young wife, Michelle, that it was he who contacted the papers. In truth, by the time he had contacted them the whole ghastly story was ready to go to the front page.

Michelle doesn't really care whether it was Sean or not, all she knows is that almost in a blink of an eye her whole life was turned upside down for the better. One minute she and little Teresa were prisoners in the top bedroom and the next minute Le Petit Manoir was invaded by reporters and a crack squad from Social Services.

Sean's mother, Dymphna O'Herlihy, stepped in to look after Michelle, at Sean's request, and Mother Nature took care of events shortly thereafter.

'Well, if I have a girl, we'll definitely have to call her Teresa.' Michelle tells Sean. Her only sadness is that, in all the mayhem that ensued when the reporters invaded the house, she lost sight of her tiny charge. She hates to think of what Miss Maitland might do to her.

25. Friendly Acres

However, Michelle's fears have proved unfounded, so far nobody has seen hide nor hair of Miss Eliza Maitland and she certainly hasn't been missed; except by the medical profession as an object of curiosity.

Le Petit Manoir is now under new management and is now "The Friendly Acres Rest Home for Retired Airport Staff". If you were to take a walk around its now immaculate grounds you might be struck by the appearance of a tree in the corner, where the owners have now fenced off a separate play area for their adopted twins, Derek and Michael.

About 12 feet tall, covered in moss and sprouting fungi around its roots, a distended abscess bulges around its trunk. One of the branches points up towards the sky like a gnarled and bony hand caught in the act. Mr. and Mrs. Graham, the new owners of the property, are thinking of having it chopped down by the tree surgeon. But for the moment are content to let the boys use the tree for target practice, as long as they don't alarm the elderly residents or upset the neighbours.

26. Helping hands

The lovely Wendy Allen, the nurse from Bluebell Ward took an interest in all of the children from Le Petit Manoir. She and Mrs. Graham worked together and arranged for a foster family to take on both Denise and Kevin, so they need never be separated.

Shelley and Julie are now in a nice new progressive children's home, where they can call the staff by their first names. They are both now intending to be nurses and have picked Health and Social Care as one of their options at school. They are also taking it in turns to get their revenge on men, by mercilessly pursuing all the teenage boys in the children's home. The tables have been turned.

As for Ian, he has been offered an Apprenticeship with a newspaper in London, apparently he has a unique skill set, which his mentor, Ms. Brinsden, says is greatly in demand in undercover reporting.

27.Little Sylvia

Sergeant Pete and his wife, Annie, often take long strolls in the forest. They are like a young married couple again, Pete is thinking of cutting back his hours and spending more time at home, now that they have a young one to look after. After all little Sylvia will soon be starting school. She looks nothing like either him or his wife, with that long brown hair, tanned skin and those big green eyes.
'If anyone ever asks, just tell them that your mum had Gypsies on her side of the family.' says Sergeant Pete.
Annie Woods rolls her eyes heavenwards, mum would have "loved" that!

My Father's Suitcase
by
Lizzie Jarrett

My Father's Suitcase

Friday April 3rd 2020 20.45

The weather-worn and battered brown case lay there innocuously.
'Now then Miss, I'd like you to repeat to my colleague what you just told me'.
The woman looked nervously around, as if seeking some kind of approval, before she opened her mouth.
'Well officer, it's like this…'

***

Twelve months earlier

1. Gene-Netix

"Gene-Netix; welcome to the future! At the forefront of Genetic Research our flagship facilities in Newbridge are helping to shape and transform the way we understand the Human Genome. Gene-Netix is the leading name in Gene Technology and we are the number one destination for research scientists from around the world. Come with us on a journey into tomorrow with the best and most enquiring minds of today…."

Jenny Cooper, large and lanky, unsung and unloved, had been beavering away at Gene-Netix for ten years since she left university. She had sacrificed a lot for this job and had been rewarded with a highly-paid position; earning twice as much as her parents could have ever dreamed of.

There *were* some things she regretted, one of which was breaking up with Paul Thomas, her boyfriend from the 6th form; he had gone on to marry that God-awful Sharon Smedley. Jenny was also starting to feel rather broody; having seen many of her friends from school settled down with families of their own. However, she did have the satisfaction of …. "What did she have the satisfaction of.. ?" she wondered to herself, as a vague and disappointed frown appeared on her face.

2. Inspiration

It was her coffee break at work, although, strictly speaking, this was inaccurate since Jenny was, and always would be, a tea drinker; coffee made her head spin. Jenny sipped her tea slowly out of the reinforced cardboard cup. The cardboard made her top lip stick to the edge of the cup, which irritated her, but she realised she was doing her bit for the environment because it was fully recyclable; it said so on the bottom of the cup.

Suddenly everything went into slow-motion as Jenny noticed, out of the corner of her eye, someone and something, at first glance, small and insignificant. It was "Bring your child to work day" today. She watched as a small red-headed girl trailed behind her red-headed father, as he caught the lift to the fourth floor.

Jenny often found herself looking longingly at fathers and daughters, hoping to detect the connections and similarities between them. Maybe this was because she had been denied so many precious years with her own father. In this case the little girl, who she was now staring at, was the mirror image of the father, there could never be any doubt that they were closely related.

Whatever it was about the father and child, Jenny couldn't tell you even now, but suddenly everything seemed to crystallise in front of her eyes. She had spent the last two years at Gene-Netix trying to justify her hypothesis on the inheritance of recessive genes; *"Mendelian inheritance thinking; the next steps."*, but there in front of her hanging in the air, as if written by an other-worldly hand, was the correct answer to her calculations.

She quickly swigged back her tea and returned to her workstation in the main laboratory on the ground floor. Turning to her computer, she brought up on-screen her last few calculations. Now, with renewed vigour and inspiration, she quickly saw the mistake she had been making over the last few years. She changed one column of calculations completely and suddenly her whole research hypothesis fitted into place, as if by divine intervention.

Out from under her desk she pulled her faithful briefcase and stuffed her latest printout inside the lining of the case. She didn't know why, but she also downloaded all of her research onto a memory stick and then placed this inside the lining of the case, alongside the printout. If only she had known then how much she would come to regret this decision.

With a little chuckle of excitement Jenny set off for home extra, extra early. She would make up the time at some point in the future, she reasoned to herself. In her mind's eye she saw herself standing on the podium as she was announced as the guest speaker at next year's world Genetics conference in Copenhagen. She saw handsome research scientists queuing up to be introduced to her, she saw her boss handing her a huge pay rise.... Yes, now was the time to buy herself some Champagne and celebrate her miraculous breakthrough. Her boss, the handsome and, as yet, unmarried Martin Fletcher, could congratulate her later. Maybe he would take out to dinner and then…who knows?

Swinging her case gaily alongside her she exited the building. Because she worked for a research company she had to go through security checks to exit the building. Unloved and ignored she may have been by many, however Barry, the security guard, still had a soft spot for her. Since he was a little too interested in patting Jenny down as she left the premises, his very cursory inspection of her briefcase revealed nothing other than a rather uninspiring packed lunch, a used gym kit and a pair of size 8 trainers all stuffed inside a supermarket carrier bag.

Once outside Jenny popped the trainers on, put her work shoes in the plastic bag instead, and walked off towards the train station.

3.Janusz

She was extremely devoted to the case, it had been through more adventures than Jenny herself was aware of. Her dad, Janusz, had left Poland in 1947 with a fervent wish never to return. He had brought with him a small brown suitcase, the only possession he had been allowed at the time. The only memento Jenny now had of her father was the case. Just small enough to go on a plane as in-flight baggage, it was now her trusty companion. It was also the perfect size to fit her gym kit and some sandwiches.

From her father's experiences during the 2nd World War, Jenny had taken one salient fact: never trust anyone. It was from him that she had inherited the idea of hiding anything valuable inside the lining of the case. It was more than a lining, it was more of a de facto secret compartment.

When the allied forces had found Janusz he had been chained to the floor of an SS special detainment camp for political prisoners. He had spent the next few years trying to rehabilitate himself in Poland, but in the end took advantage of a resettlement programme and came to England.

The war had taken its toll and Janusz Kopelski never truly recovered. It was purely by chance that Janusz, now in his seventies, became the object of affection of Jenny's mother, Christine. It had truly been a May-December romance and Jenny had been the result. After a short period of relative sanity, her father's war demons returned to haunt him and he returned to the bottom of the whiskey bottle. So now the only reminder that she had was her father's suitcase: battered, brown and covered with dents and scratches.

4. The long journey home

By now she was on the train back home. It was a hot day and she had found herself nodding off. The mini bottle of Champagne she had bought herself from the mini-mart next to the station was doing its job. First her eyes felt heavy, her chin touched her chest and she was off into dreamland.

The brown case that she had clasped defensively between her knees tipped over and fell at the feet of someone far less well-intentioned and deserving than this lonely, single scientist from Sussex.

Jay Watkiss is on his way home too, but the battered brown case has caught his eye. He is tiny for his age and he often uses this to his advantage, pretending to be younger than he is. He certainly looks like he should be back in school. With his cute dimples and his over-sized mouth; he smiles beatifically at ticket collectors, shop assistants and anyone else who might mistake him for a child.

Jay wonders what might be inside Jenny's case. He is not a novice to this game, he knows that the case itself is of no value to him, but he thinks the contents might be. Sneakily and slowly he opens the case and empties the contents into his sports bag. He then gets off the train at the very next stop without Jenny being any the wiser. However, our dozy heroine just sleeps on, as if she were a princess poisoned by a sleeping draught.

Jenny would usually catch the fast train home, but since this is the middle of the day the train is stopping at every single little station. The kind of station that Jenny has only ever seen in a blur, as the fast train rushed through. It is now slowing down again and pulling into Rentham station. Rentham is famous for only two things; being the birthplace of Oliver Martindale, a little-known Romantic poet of the 1820s, but primarily it is known for being the site of the largest Young Offenders Institution in the South of England.

"Rentham Young Offenders Institution is located just south of London. Originally built in the early 1860s as an Industrial School for the poor and neglected children of South London. The current institution was re-opened

officially by the Prisons Minister in 1990. In order to help transform the lives and the behaviour of the inmates one of the many aims of the institution was to offer a skill and a trade for each young inmate. However, recent reports have suggested that this has been largely unsuccessful. There is a high degree of violence amongst inmates and recidivism of paroled inmates is high.
Interim report: The Hewson League for Penal Reform, May 2018"

It is here that Jenny's father's suitcase was to suffer further indignities. Preston and Thatcher Waites are just out of Rentham this afternoon where they have learned no helpful lessons whatsoever, nor learned any useful skills. They are certainly not here to make friends or pay for train tickets.

These boys are a disappointment to their parents, Karl and Tracey; who have worked every hour God sends to give their twin sons a stable and pleasant home life. But it seems that the best endeavours of respectable people are sometimes not enough. Preston and Thatcher have taken everything their parents have ever given them and thrown it back in their faces. Stoked up on whatever is the drug of the moment, this skin-headed, acne-skinned pair run through the train yelling at the passengers in other carriages and causing mayhem. But still Jenny sleeps on.

Arriving in Jenny's carriage, where she is now the sole occupant the two boys come momentarily to a halt as they both look at the suitcase. Preston looks at Thatcher, as if to say 'I dare you!'. Without a second thought Thatcher picks up the case and throws it out of the window. Having made their pathetic protest the lads run on through to the next carriage and jump off at the next station. What a day they are having!

5. Separate ways

The case falls down an embankment and eventually comes to rest in a bed of leaves. It begins to rain heavily. On the train Jenny is awoken by the crack of thunder and streaks of lightning. She looks down for the case and finds to her distress that it is gone!

Somewhere in a dingy flat in Croydon Jay Watkiss is emptying out his spoils of the day and is disappointed to find it contains a plastic supermarket bag in which is a pair of rather smelly high-heeled shoes, a used gym kit and some hummus sandwiches. He's definitely had better hauls.

Meanwhile the battered brown suitcase sits all on its own at the bottom of the embankment, getting wetter and wetter.

Night soon closes in and the suitcase sits camouflaged in the leaf mould. It is the perfect shelter for the night for a small hedgehog who comes truffling past, crunching on his most recent meal of worms and woodlice. A badger emerges briefly from the undergrowth only to retreat as an oncoming BMW announces its arrival with full fog lights and the muffled thump-thump-thump of the driver's heavy metal playlist. By one o'clock in the morning the rain starts to clear up and the quiet country road returns to silence again.

6. The Eco-Warrior

The pale and watery sun rises over the soggy landscape and the early morning traffic starts afresh. First the postman arrives, then the early morning delivery drivers, but then there is one solitary and lonely pedestrian, Jerry Pettit. He is quite a character. He has travelled across the South of England, sleeping in the bushes and barns and occasionally accepting the offer of a bed for the night from well-intentioned strangers. Jerry is something of a modern-day preacher, an eco-warrior, call it what you will. But today he is the recipient of a free suitcase sent to him from the railway Gods. It is just the right size, it is completely free and his army-surplus rucksack had just broken. He needs something to put his rather scant possessions in.

He pulls out of his pocket a screwed up poster that he has been sent by the local protest group.

"Fight the Frackers !

Meeting on Saturday 6th April at 3pm, Slaughterfield Village Hall

Speaker and eco-campaigner, Jerry Pettit will give the keynote speech. Listen to what he has to say about the future and safety of your village and its beautiful surroundings.

Don't believe the government's lies!

The future of Slaughterfield is in your hands!

Tea and Coffee will be served after the meeting."

Jerry is due to speak at Slaughterfield village hall. Eurofrack, a conglomerate company concerned with extracting oil and gas deposits are planning to sink some test shafts just outside Slaughterfield. Jerry is the unlikely poster-boy for the protest campaign.

He received an invitation via the protest network from a "Sally-Anne Walter" at Wisteria Cottage. He has been invited to stay the night in her guest bedroom after the meeting.

Sally-Anne Walter does indeed live in a beautiful Wisteria covered cottage. She is the youngest daughter of Major Mycroft-Mallett and his wife, Lise. The Mycroft-Mallets live at Slaughterfield Hall, whilst their children are scattered around the village living in tied cottages. With no real wish, nor need, nor indeed any known ability to make money, Sally-Anne is able to use her position in society to devote her life to eco-causes. She really admires Jerry Pettit, she thinks he is akin to a saint.

7. Beautiful Slaughterfield

"Slaughterfield is a village within the Wealden District of East Sussex, England. It is located eight miles (13 km) east of Westbourne in the valley north of the South Downs. The Slaughterfield valley was formed by the Slaughter river. The dramatic scenery has been the inspiration for many artists, but in recent times has become the backdrop to a long-running battle between Eurofrack, an oil and gas company, and various protest groups who oppose their extraction methods.

The village is mentioned in the Domesday Book and has had a number of names, including Slafterfeld, Slort and also just plain Slaughter. The 13th-century parish church is dedicated to St. Aethelred, the Warrior King. There is one public house, The Red Ensign. There is limited public transport to and from the village.

Excerpt from 'The Towns and Villages of Sussex' by Nadia Gorringe, available at all good booksellers."

Round the corner, several hours earlier than Sally-Anne was expecting him, comes Jerry. Sally-Anne finds herself having to make some re-adjustments. Her eco-hero is slightly older than she had imagined him to be and is definitely and dangerously in need of a bath. Nevertheless her association with him can only help her credentials amongst the other local eco-warriors, including Jason Halliwell, scion of the Halliwell clan. Unlike Jerry, Jason is devastatingly attractive, young, currently unattached and also heir to a fortune of several million. More importantly the more Sally-Anne associates with these "eco-types", the more it will completely annoy "Daddy".

8. Daddy!

" Slaughterfield Hall looks backwards in so many ways. Inconveniently located on the north-facing slopes of the South Downs, the Hall is both draughty and cold throughout the year. Designed and constructed in the mid 1600s by the little known architect, Grange Gall; the building has, what can only be described as, a Spartan aesthetic. In recent years there have been attempts to market the Hall as a wedding venue, it is understood this venture has met with little success. The current family, the Mycroft-Mallets, are descendants of Admiral "Bruffy" Mycroft-Mallet, who inherited the hall as part of a gambling debt in the early 1800s.

Excerpt from the 'Notable homes of Sussex by Gloria Pullinger'. Available at all good booksellers."

Major "Bronco" Mycroft-Mallet is, at this very moment, in his bedroom doing his early morning calisthenics. His very impressive, but rather chilly house, Slaughterfield Hall, sits at the top of a hill. It has a commanding view over Slaughterfield valley and the local river, the Slaughter. Picking up

a pair of binoculars that he keeps on his bedside table he peers down towards his daughter's house.
'I see Sally-Anne is making a fool of herself again.' he remarks to his wife.
'Yes dear' says Lise, as she rolls over in bed in the forlorn hope of getting back to sleep.

Out of the corner of her eye she examines her husband. This once handsome man, who had captured her heart and her country during World War II, was now a quirky little caricature of a British army officer. Stick-thin, but still with all the poise of a military man, he stood there in his Y-fronts and his string vest, binoculars in hand.
'You should leave her alone, you know' his wife went on, 'nothing good will come of this obsession of yours.'

Some years ago the Mycroft-Mallets had used their army connections and a hefty financial incentive to push their wayward daughter into a marriage with Colonel "Mad Mike" Walter's son, Peter. The whole thing had ended in tears and now Sally-Anne fills her empty days befriending lost sheep and trying to impress, usually, much younger men of the hairy, grungy, eco-warrior persuasion. Her two children, Kit and Scarlett, are away at boarding school and scarcely ever try to make contact with her.

9. Wisteria Cottage

But it is into Sally-Anne's cosy cottage that Jerry Petitt finds himself invited today.
'Do make yourself at home in the bathroom. I've put some fresh flannels and towels in there. I'll be having lunch at one o'clock at The Red Ensign, you're welcome to join me there before we have our meeting in the village hall'.
Jerry looks at his host, she is pretty much what he had expected. Mid 30s, about 5 foot 7, scrawny with blonded hair and dressed in designer "grunge" gear. She could have been straight out of central casting for the character of "very well-off pseudo eco-warrior". But Jerry is very, very glad that he can use her shower.

"Days out in Ye Olde Sussex

Customers are in for a treat when they visit The Red Ensign in Slaughterfield. Dating back to the 16th Century The Red Ensign offers that traditional "olde-world" Sussex experience. Snuggle up next to one of the pub's two traditional ingle-nook fireplaces. Gaze at the oak beams and wonder what conversations have taken place here in the centuries before. The origin of the name is thought to date back to the formation of the British flag....

Excerpt from 'The Towns and Villages of Sussex' by Nadia Gorringe, available at all good booksellers."

The writer of this review might have been taken aback to find that the origin of the pub's name actually dates back to *Star Trek* and not the British flag. Janice, the landlord's wife and top Star Trek fan girl, used the name as a bargaining chip when she and Alfie took over the pub.

Alfie drew the line at Janice's plans for the interior of the pub, she was thinking more along the lines of a Starship Enterprise theme pub. Whereas in a happy compromise that marks every really successful marriage, Janice has had to content herself with letting Alfie have free rein over the pub interior. This is why it is packed to the rafters with country curios; cheesemakers, harnesses, horseshoes and any other rural nick-nack that Alfie can get his hands on. Continuing its contradictory themes, The Red Ensign is also well-known locally for its "Vegan Favourites" selection. So Jerry and Sally-Anne are able to fill their stomachs and salve their consciences at the same time, as they tuck into chilli and vegan cheese fries which accompany their beetroot burgers.

The clientele appear to be mostly prosperous upper-middle class Sussex folk. There are a few mummies and daddies struggling to control their "lovely" children who are home from prep. school for the weekend, a couple of farmers propping up the bar and a few local accountants and estate agents who are enjoying their precious weekends away from their offices. The Red Ensign is always a good choice for those hoping to escape to the country for the weekend.

10. Out of towners

But today there are some interlopers, drug dealers from nearby Angelbridge posing as accountants. They have come to do a deal with Sally-Anne's latest crush, Jason Halliwell.

'Leave the gear behind the counter with Alfie, you'll see a battered leather suitcase near the bar, take that. The cash will be inside.' These are the instructions that they have received over the phone from Jason.

Richie Morrison and Chelsea Lee are posing as an accountant and accounts clerk. Chelsea has even gone to the trouble of inventing a back story and is enjoying her day out in the country. It makes a change from Angelbridge, the town that time forgot. Richie is getting quite edgy, this is his big chance to impress his dad, Derek, the local drugs kingpin of Angelbridge. He feels honoured to have been given this very important task. Chelsea, his girlfriend, is beginning to get on his nerves. She's been rabbiting on about the purchase ledger and the sales ledger for several hours now, in her role as "Tracey Jones - Accounts Clerk". Richie just wants to get the suitcase and go. Suddenly he spies it.
'There it is Chels', let's get it and go.'
They surprise Alfie, the barman, by giving him a supermarket bag of used £50 notes. Alfie doesn't argue and Richie and Chelsea emerge, blushing and flustered, into the sunlight outside.

Unbeknownst to the two of them, Jason Halliwell is not even in Slaughterfield today; he has absented himself. But he did tell his friends, Terry and Tom, in the flying squad that the deal would be going down today. Jason Halliwell is a very lazy daddy's boy, but he finds that being a police informer earns him plenty of dosh without the need for any real work.

Sitting outside in the Beer Garden, pretending to sip Lager, are Terry and Tom, dressed up for the day as eco-campaigners. Terry, in particular, feels a right twat. As he left for work today he had already changed into his "eco-gear".
'What the hell are you wearing?' said Jean, his wife.
'Don't ask love, you don't want to know!' came her husband's terse reply.

11. Separate ways once more

As Richie goes past, brown battered suitcase in hand, Tom sticks out his foot and Richie falls flat on the ground. The case, needing little encouragement, pops open revealing nothing more than a very dirty pair of Jerry's pants and a very well-loved toothbrush. Back in the pub Jerry Petitt enjoys a second pint of "The Captain's Special" and is oblivious to the theft of his recently acquired case. The day's not going well for Sally-Anne either, she was hoping she would catch sight of Jason and he is nowhere to be seen.

Terry secures his prisoners in the back of the unmarked police car and Tom marches into the pub to collect the plastic bag of evidence from behind the bar. Good old Alfie, what a stand-up guy, and retired under-cover police officer, he is.

The suitcase gets flung unceremoniously into the boot. As far as Terry and Tom are concerned, they have done their job; they have retrieved an agreed empty suitcase and a bag of money from the pub. The bank notes will have all the forensic evidence they need. Terry laughs to himself, it was a nice touch, the dirty underwear and the toothbrush! Deep inside the lining of the case, Jenny's print out and memory stick sit, undisturbed and unsullied.

12. April again - twelve months later

Jenny Cooper often wonders to herself what has become of her briefcase. Her "nicking off" early on the day of the "great breakthrough" had not gone down well with her boss, Martin Fletcher. He's only concerned with what is commercially viable. Jenny rabbited on about her findings, but unfortunately the strain of their loss, and the fact that she had absolutely no scientific data forthcoming meant that the company now saw Jenny as a liability. She has now been given her marching orders from Gene-Netix. With only her cat to talk to, she now cuts a lonely and sad figure.

She has very little money available so she often spends her days scanning the small ads of her local paper in the hope of something cheap and cheerful to entertain her.

*"Friday 3rd April
Town Hall
7pm
Police Auction. All proceeds to go to the St. Athelstan's Hedgehog Sanctuary.
'Let's be having you down to Town Hall for an auction of items no longer of interest to the boys in blue. You'll be arrested by the sight of what we've got in store for you.'*

*Saturday 4th April
7pm Gilbert and Sullivan's The Mikado by the Harold's Heath players".*

With nothing else to lose Jenny gets the bus down to the local Town Hall. She takes a chair at the back of the hall and the auction starts.
'Ladies and Gentlemen, what am I bid for this delightful pair of ornamental elephant plant pots?....a beautiful brooch, silver effect with an amethyst coloured stone...'

At the end of the evening there is a feature called "Anything goes!". It is a selection of some less than prestigious lots grouped together.
'Ladies and Gentlemen, what will you give me for this job lot?'
Jenny stares and then stares again. Right in front of her, as clear as day, is her father's suitcase.

'That's mine!' she yells.
The auctioneer looks at her incredulously.
'No really, it belongs to me.' Jenny protests, she feels herself gasping, as if she were a fish stranded on the bank of a river.
'How much will you give me for the lot, after all it is for charity?' says the auctioning officer.
'I've got a fiver.' Jenny shouts out in desperation.
'Sold, to the lady in the green coat!'.

In shock Jenny edges towards the stage, with shaking hands, to reclaim her prized possession. As she reaches the stage she is unable to contain herself and she blurts out the whole sorry tale to Sergeant Terry Pritchard. At the end of her story the Sergeant puts his hand out in congratulation and gesturing to his colleague, Tom, who has just returned from the refreshments area with two cups of coffee, he says.

'Now then Miss, I'd like you to repeat to my colleague what you just told me'.
The woman looked nervously around, as if seeking some kind of approval, before she opened her mouth.
'Well officer, it's like this…'.

The Cutting Room Floor
by
Lizzie Jarrett

The Cutting Room Floor

1.

"Artificia Productions bring you their ground-breaking production of The Crucible. Star of ITV's "General Practice", Stevie Bright, brings us his unique and powerful interpretation of John Proctor. Performing opposite him in the role of Abigail Williams will be Michaela Prince, known to BBC viewers in her role as Rainy Daze from the hit show "Rainy and the Rockettes"

From a place of privilege and entitlement a stupid man set out upon his stupid day. His head was full of minor plans and inconsequentialities, which had no place in the head of anyone in any position of power. However, as is so often the case, power and opportunity is not always given to those that truly deserve it; sometimes the ball of chance can be caught by literally *anyone*. Such was the case with Stevie Bright; always in the right place at the right time, smiling his inane smile at everyone and anyone. A grinning clown of a man; his face bore the same expression whatever day of the year it was and whichever way the wind was blowing. Luck always seemed to favour him.

From the very beginning his mother had fostered in her son this unstoppable self-belief. When he had been born she had dropped all other distractions and funnelled all of her energies into this grateful, but vacuous sponge. But now, for the first time in his life, the opinions of others were no longer in tune with those of his mother and certainly were not quite so kind.

"THE GOOLE ADVERTISER
An ill-advised production of The Crucible hit town this week, starring the featherweight talent of Stevie Bright in the heavyweight role of John Proctor. His paper-thin acting was not up to the rigours of this play, famously written by Arthur Miller…..

THE BEXHILL TIMES
….this production is truly dire, everyone involved should be truly ashamed…

THE LINCOLN GAZETTE
The local secondary school put on the same play last year, it was infinitely superior….

THE PETERSFIELD HERALD
Michaela Prince should have thought twice before accepting the role of the teenager, Abigail Williams. She is still a great actress but she is definitely no spring chicken…."

Stevie Bright, in comparison with Michaela Prince, was an actor of dubious talent, often playing the leading or title role. He was now decidedly past his prime. But rather than accept the friendly hints dropped by well-meaning friends and acquaintances, he had set up his own theatre company; so that he was simultaneously the producer, the director and, of course, the romantic lead.

2.

As is the way with many theatre companies Stevie felt happy in the company of his own friends; so an "Artificia" production might well feature the same merry band of familiar faces, year in, year out.

Artificia's stage company toured the provinces, setting on fire the hearts of many a lady of a certain age. It had been a profitable little business, but with Stevie increasingly unable to take a back seat, reviews were starting to turn ugly and takings at the box office were down.

'What about getting me my own TV series again, something along the lines of "Murder in Martinique" would be great', Stevie enthused to Janice Pullet, his PA, 'I could solve a different murder every week, we could film the whole thing on location.'

Janice Pullet was efficient, some would say ruthless, in her pursuit of whatever Stevie needed or desired. There was definitely a suspicion that Janice had more access to Stevie's bank account than his wife did. But even she knew that Stevie's star was no longer bright enough to fund the "Murder in Martinique" idea. There was certainly no way the BBC or ITV would entertain such a fancy.

That is how she found herself as financial director and PA for Stevie's latest venture, his own film company, "Artificially Bright". One day they are plying their trade in arts centres across the country, the next Stevie Bright is to be producer, director and romantic lead of Romeo and Juliet, the company's first venture on celluloid.

Playing opposite him in the role of Juliet would be Michaela Prince, perhaps she could lend the production the gravitas it needs. Stevie would frequently star opposite Michaela, a talented actress in her own right. They had, in fact, been an item at secondary school, before Stevie had singled out someone with significantly less confidence and good looks than himself to be his future wife and bearer of his children. Michaela didn't waste any time mourning over their dead romance, she had married and divorced two husbands already. She was now content simply to have a younger man around, who would make himself available at her beck and call.

Michaela knew that by sticking with Stevie she would always have access to greater opportunities than she might have on her own account. She knew she would never have to play second fiddle to a younger model. Perhaps she really should look in the mirror a second or third time, before accepting another romantic lead. Sometimes another layer of foundation was not going to cover those ever-increasing cracks and wrinkles. No doubt on a man's face they would have called it character.

3.

From a place of relative poverty and lack of entitlement, a young man by the name of Conrad Campbell found himself weighing up the price of the supermarket "value" baked beans against the price of the beans that he actually enjoyed eating. In the same way that Stevie's mum had doted on him, Conrad's mother had left him alone in the house one day when he was 15 and run off to the Costa del Crime with her distinctly shady boyfriend.

Life has not been fair to Conrad. In the same way that Stevie had always been in the right place at the right time, life for Conrad was often one blind alley and missed opportunity after another. Still at least all his achievements were his own and not down to anyone else. Conrad mused on this thought as he threw the disgusting "value" beans into his shopping basket.

He was an energetic young man, which meant that after his mother had left he had spent the next few years getting into trouble. He had got rather too familar with the police, drinking too much and taking various interesting substances. Luckily his natural intolerance for boredom kicked in and he had found steady work as a waiter and barman and, occasionally, as a film extra.

Today he was on his way to see his agent, Georgie. She had promised him something different this time. His last "extra" job had been one month in Birchwood studios in the latest superhero film. He had been "Museum Attendant No. 3". However, as was often the case, "Museum Attendant No. 3" had ended up on the cutting room floor and whilst Conrad had got money in his pocket for the work, he was getting a little sick of the whole "extras" scene.

Running up the rickety old back stairs to Georgie's office, Conrad exploded through the door, trademark grin on his handsome young face. Georgie had been a friend of his mum's; so in a roundabout way she had eventually done something to help her son out. Unlike Conrad's mother, Georgie was of the porcelain-skinned, hennaed-hair variety of woman. She also delighted in horrifying the vegetarians, vegans and animal lovers of Helmstone by sporting a real fur coat, whatever the weather. It was a wonder she hadn't been torn to shreds in the streets.

'Dahling….how lovely to see you, as always. Well, have I got something special for you. Stevie Bright, an old, old friend of mine is filming locally. He's camped outside of "The Camellia Mansion", just near Little Retching if you know it? So, what do you think to having a small part in Romeo and Juliet?' Georgie looked engagingly across the table at the young actor.

Conrad had heard of the name Stevie Bright before. Stevie Bright was the kind of man your aunt, or perhaps your grandma, might have had a crush on. He had been the heart-throb star of "General Practice" during the 1980s. Stevie had played the role of Dr. James Everett, the sensitive doctor who saved the lives of thousands over the 10 years in which his show was a hit on TV.

Conrad took a deep breath, swallowed his pride, and asked 'Sure, sure Georgie, but how am I supposed to get there? I can't drive and there's no bus or train that goes anywhere near Little Retching.'

'Well, that's the genius of the plan. Michaela Prince, she's an old friend, told me that she would be delighted to offer a lift to any young man that needs a lift.' Georgie said, and then added cryptically 'you might enjoy the ride.'

Signed, sealed, delivered and all tied up with a little pink bow, that was exactly how Conrad felt, but he wasn't really in any position to argue.

4.

The first day of filming began and Conrad stood on the sea front awaiting his lift. A red Porsche rolled up, inside was a heavily made-up woman with blonded hair. Definitely striking once, but also at least twice his age. Her skirt was slit thigh high, whenever she pushed her foot down on the accelerator Conrad felt compelled to avert his eyes.

'So, you're Scarlett's son? Pleasure to meet you.' She pulled her sunglasses back down and off they shot along the seafront, screeching to a sudden right turn and heading off in the direction of Little Retching village. Her long red fingernails gripped the gearstick assertively, as she shifted the car into a higher gear.

5.

Little Retching is a village located 8 miles due north-west of Helmstone, a seaside town in East Sussex. It is contained within the boundaries of the Helmstone Downs National Park. It is known locally for its picturesque flint cottages and its stunning landscape.

There has been a settlement here since Anglo-Saxon times when the people of Recca first claimed the land, that may be the origin of the name. It is recorded in the Domesday book of 1089. At this time there were two smallholdings listed, between whom there were many acrimonious disputes ranging from petty-theft and sheep-rustling, but also various occurrences of maiming and manslaughter. In Tudor times a large grant of land was gifted to Henry VIII's favourites and it was at this time that a "Marquess of Billingsborough" was first listed as owning the land.

An artistic community grew up in the late 1800s around the celebrated Victorian eccentric, and co-incidentally the very last Marquess of Billingsborough, William Hurst-Clevedon, legendary dramatic performer, party-giver and party-goer. He sought to establish a cultural centre near Little Retching in which to stage theatrical spectaculars. Castle

Verona was finally built in 1893; it was designed by the flamboyant and eccentric architect, Lando Wilde, who styled the castle to mimic a mediterranean villa. The Marquess chose to have it painted in a rather striking pink shade, leading to various derogatory nicknames being given to it, "The Pink Palace" and "The Folly" being ones that are acceptable to repeat in polite society. However, it was during a party to celebrate their first season as a theatrical troupe that fire spread throughout the building reducing it to a shell. The building was never occupied again and the Marquess died shortly thereafter of a broken heart, but possibly also from the ill-effects of a rather dissolute lifestyle.

The gardens of Castle Verona, known locally as "The Camellia Mansion", still survive. The remains of the house provide a suitably stunning backdrop, featuring as they do, an amphitheatre. The National Trust are trying to raise funds to buy this house for the nation, but in the meantime it is often in demand as a spectacular location for performing arts ventures and for films. This could be seen as a fitting tribute to a remarkable man....

Excerpts from 'The Towns and Villages of Sussex' by Nadia Gorringe and 'Notable homes of Sussex' by Gloria Pullinger, both available at all good booksellers"

6.

Over the next few days Conrad got to know some of the actors and crew. Always on hand was make-up lady, "gopher" and chief cheerleader, Maureen Duffy. She had been nanny to Stevie and Penny's rather spoilt children, Sylvester and Serena. Now they no longer needed a nanny she had inveigled her way onboard ship. With no dramatic talent and with very little to call on in the way of looks, she did what she could behind-the-scenes to keep herself occupied and keep onboard the good ship "Bright". If Maureen could have been Stevie's personal secretary she would have done so, but that role had already been taken by Janice. If you ever wanted to find Stevie during the day, all you had to do was look for Maureen because she was his virtual shadow.

Janice Pullet, Stevie's PA, was a desiccated raisin of a woman, stick-thin and with a permed mane of hair; which gave her the appearance of being a human lollipop. She was there to make sure everything Stevie wanted, Stevie got. Conrad was stunned at how little dignity two middle-aged ladies could display in pursuit of the good opinion of one singularly untalented middle-aged man; who had merely had the good fortune to have starred in a successful television programme nearly 30 years ago.

There was a small cheery rounded woman called Wendy-Jane Hughes, who was playing the role of the Nurse. If she was perplexed at how on earth she was playing Nurse to a woman who was at least the same age as her, she had the good grace not to show it. A bearded, balding man by the name of Lawrence O'Halloran was, appropriately enough, playing the part of Friar Lawrence. At least Lawrence was a good actor, which made up for the distinct lack of talent shown by the leading man.

A grumpy Scottish cameraman, Andrew McAllister, who had actually won an Oscar earlier on his career, worked his magic on the shooting of the sets. If only they could have cast the same spell over the two "star actors". There are only so many layers of panstick that the march of time can cover and only so much "Only for men" hair dye that could be used on Stevie's grey hairs. Only Stevie Bright's most die-hard fans were going to pay to see this film. It needed a little bit of publicity, it needed to be on the front page.

The next few days were pretty much what Conrad had come to expect; he got into make-up and full Shakespearian togs and then sat patiently awaiting for a scene involving him for the next 12 hours. The highlight of the day was the thrilling Porsche ride home. Every day Michaela would arrive in a new and totally inappropriate outfit. The hemlines rose ever higher and the cleavage descended yet lower and lower, one day soon they would meet in the middle.

7.

At the end of the 3rd day Michaela made her move.
'Why not stop off for a drink on the way home or even come round to my house?' she said, in what was quite definitely a seductive tone.

Conrad managed to fend off her advances this time, but as he arrived back at his flat that evening the smell of a 5 day old curry and several days beer consumption hit him. It wasn't as though he were completely blameless, he had partaken of the curry and bloody nice it was too. The beer had washed down the curry nicely, however sharing a flat with four other blokes wasn't ideal whenever he had wanted to bring a girl home. Perhaps he shouldn't have had so much pride, he bet Michaela didn't have a flat share arrangement. She sure as hell didn't content herself with a 5 day old curry and flat beer.

8.

The very next day Conrad and the rest of the company were treated to a truly stomach-churning love scene between Stevie and Michaela. The lack of self-awareness of the two central players was utterly staggering. By mid-morning there was a break and the stars retired to their trailers. Everyone had been expected back on set by 11.30, even those not involved in the next scene. But "Romeo" himself had not re-emerged from his trailer, so a call was made for a runner to go and fetch him. However, in their general disorganisation "Artificially Bright's" runner had let them down that morning, so the job fell to Conrad.
'Just go and knock on the trailer door and wake him up' said Michaela.

Arriving at the trailer Conrad found the door closed, after knocking for the 3rd time and still with no answer he tried the door. He had never been into one of these mobile "trailer-palaces" before. It was immaculate, he certainly would have swapped this for No. 26 Victory Terrace any day.

However, spoiling the magnolia calm of the interior was a bundle of velvet collapsed on the floor. Underneath the red velvet cloak, which had fallen in a rather undignified manner over the actor's face, was the contorted body of Stevie Bright.
'Oh God!' said Conrad.
As he stumbled back out of the trailer he stepped backwards onto the hem of Michaela Prince's yellow velvet dress.

'Oh my God!' cried Michaela, unintentionally echoing Conrad's first reaction, 'run back to the set and tell them what's happened' she commanded.
Without a second thought Conrad turned tail and ran back to the set, where the restless company had assembled.

The screaming that issued from the mouth of Maureen Duffy was ear-shatteringly loud. Stevie Bright's number one fan was truly devastated. The reaction of Stevie's wife, when she arrived, was almost muted in comparison.

In all the hubbub, Wendy-Jane Hughes at least had the presence of mind to call an ambulance.

9.

Detective Inspector Jonathan March, based in nearby Billingsborough, had been contemplating taking the afternoon off and taking his young daughter, Imogen, to ride her pony at the stables. His plans were therefore thwarted when the call came in from "The Camellia Mansion".

His colleague, Constable Taylor, handed him the receiver with the words,
'Dodgy death of thespian, Sir. The ambulance crew are *not* happy and want you on the scene'.

Maybe he should have been more ambitious, maybe he should have been pleased that there had been an unexpected death that he could investigate. But for D.I. March it really was just a tiresome interruption to an otherwise lovely day.

On arriving at the scene the Inspector was met by an irate bearded and balding actor who was playing the role of Friar Lawrence.

Lawrence O'Halloran had been a talented actor in his youth, but had fallen on what he took to be hard times. He was mortified to have been taking work from the likes of Stevie Bright. Having once played Hamlet at the Young Vic he rarely let his fellow actors forget it. In truth his irritation today was fuelled by the thought of this "event" getting into the newspapers. Thus his association with Stevie's company would be unearthed in a way which he took to be undignified.

Having got little real sense out of "Friar Lawrence", Inspector March asked to be directed to the scene of the crime; where he was confronted by a frizzy haired, dough-faced woman who was still trembling with shock.
'Are you the deceased's wife?' enquired the Inspector.
'No, she's over there' said a tiny barrel-shaped woman, dressed as Juliet's nurse.

Stevie's wife, Penny, was sitting calmly on her own, dabbling delicately at her lipstick with a handkerchief. Cursory enquiries with Mrs. Bright quickly concluded themselves, when it became evident that she was nowhere near the scene of the crime.

So it was that the rest of the company took it in turns to be questioned by the Inspector and his reliable Constable, to ascertain their movements that morning. Conrad was a person of interest because he had found the body, but he was quickly dismissed when Michaela Prince was able to give him a good alibi.

10.

Things went very differently for Maureen Duffy. Faithful to the last, she had prepared Stevie his cup of coffee that morning and that cup was now material evidence in a murder case. At the end of a very exhausting day, the whole cast and crew were summoned together and told to make themselves available for more questioning at 9am on the following morning. Maureen left red-eyed and sobbing in the back of a police car.

"THE DAILY ECHO

UNEXPECTED DEATH OF '80s TELEVISION ACTOR

After the sudden death of Stevie Bright, during the filming of the Shakespearian tragedy Romeo and Juliet in Sussex, police were called to the scene and a member of the company has been taken in for questioning…

THE HELMSTONE HERALD

HOSPITAL HEART-THROB DEAD!

Police were called to "The Camellia Mansion" in Sussex yesterday when Stevie Bright failed to turn up on set during filming of Romeo and Juliet. Readers will remember Stevie from his hit series in the 1980s, General Practice, in which he played Dr. James Everett. Mr. Bright was later found to have died of causes as yet unknown…"

11.

At the end of the week Michaela summoned everyone together to make an announcement.
'OK, call me callous, call me heartless, but I've had a meeting with Penny, Stevie's widow, and we've decided that the show must go on. So please come in on Monday morning, recasting will take place then. I will attempt to replace the void created by Stevie's demise and therefore will take over as director'.

Monday morning came and the cast re-assembled. Maureen Duffy had been detained for further questioning; since the cup of coffee she had provided Stevie with had traces of anti-freeze in it. Without Maureen present the cast had to do their own make-up; the difference was imperceptible.

Michaela was determined to carry on in the role of Juliet. 'It was what Stevie would have wanted..', she said. Whilst in the role of Romeo would be that up and coming talented young actor.....Conrad Campbell!

Conrad could simultaneously see both sides of the coin here. He would immediately be thrust into the limelight, in a highly paid role and any publicity is good publicity right? On the negative side, however, he would be playing a romantic role opposite a woman clearly old enough to be his mother. As an actor he could clearly see that the "any publicity" argument easily won the day. He clung desperately to this belief over the next few days, when he found himself rehearsing love scenes with Michaela.

12.

Not that he had any great love for Stevie, he had been a pompous, talentless fool, but there was something plaguing Conrad. A little thought that went on niggling him at the back of his mind. It was something to do with the circumstances in which Conrad had found Stevie; he couldn't quite put his finger on what it was.

It was bothering someone else too. Janice Pullet had always been a little bit more than in love with Stevie. But without Stevie around Janice found herself to be virtually redundant.

The tabloid journalists who had arrived to cover the murder had stayed around. Now the headlines were different, the redoubtable Michaela Prince was the heroine of the hour. The Daily Echo echoed "We've got to carry on, it's what Stevie would have wanted", whilst The Helmstone Herald trumpeted "This film will be our tribute to a great artiste".

Janice now had a lot of spare time on her hands, she found herself preoccupied with the circumstances of Stevie's death. Something didn't add up. There was no rationale for Maureen killing

Stevie, she adored him. If only she could figure out what it was that was *so* wrong.

Her status was now so diminished, that one of her duties now was to make the mid-morning tea and coffee. She had just served the 11am refreshments, as she turned to go back to her tiny trailer there was an almighty scream from behind her. She turned round to see Michaela clutching her throat and retching, a cup which had contained coffee was lying empty in front of her. Needless to say the rest of the refreshments went untouched.

13.

Once again the police were called and the Inspector was once again met by the bearded, balding monk, rolling his eyes and complaining bitterly, yet secretly loving the extra publicity even an attempted murder would command.

The coffee cup was once again retrieved as evidence and filming stopped for the day. Michaela was rushed to hospital to undergo tests.

"Entertainment X-tra!

Speculation is rife once more on the set of the beleaguered "Artificially Bright" production of Romeo and Juliet; previously directed by, and starring, Stevie Bright. An attempt was made to poison the new director, Michaela Prince; who is also starring as Juliet. Sources told our reporter "Most people were already bringing in their own food and drink...you feel like you can't trust anyone". One of the camera team commented "I'll be glad to get this film in the can, I'm going back home to Scotland after this'.."

Once again the cast was assembled, minus Michaela of course, and this time Janice was taken away for questioning.

Conrad now had no hope that filming would ever recommence, surely with one murder and one attempted murder this film could not continue?

A few days off gave his mind time to breathe, to put things together, to assemble the building blocks. Once again he still couldn't make sense of it all. He was therefore stunned on the very next Monday morning to find himself standing on the seafront once again waiting for Michaela to take him back to the scene of the crime(s).

14.

Before filming started a very fit and happy looking Michaela took time to address the whole cast and crew.
'Thank goodness I'm a "super-taster". I had one sip of that coffee and I knew something was wrong...only think what could have happened...' and as she spoke tears welled up in her eyes. 'Anyway', she continued 'once again we are going to have to make adjustments, now that two of our merry band are suspects in a murder case. I will be

having one-to-one meetings with all cast and crew members to discuss these matters'.

First of all "Friar Lawrence" went for his meeting, he seemed mightily pleased with himself when he re-emerged.

The meetings were to be held in Stevie's old trailer, since that was no longer of interest to the police. It was as Conrad stepped through the doorway that he felt the blood drain away from him. He knew what was wrong, it wasn't the coffee in either case, it was the cups!

When he had arrived to find Stevie collapsed on the floor he had been clutching a pink coffee cup, but whenever Maureen made the coffee she had used Stevie's own cup, which was blue. When Michaela had been poisoned, the strangely empty cup that had been thrown to the ground was pink too. It wasn't Maureen or Janice, they were both far too doting. It was someone who was now sitting in front of him and had been a principal witness to the murder and who was a very, very good actress.

As he was processing all these thoughts he looked up at Michaela, who was cradling a pink cup of herbal tea in her hands. The coffee that had allegedly been made by Janice had never even touched Michaela's lips; she didn't even drink coffee.

Juliet, suddenly looked a lot more like Lady Macbeth, with her long red fingernails tapped idly on the side of the cup.

'Have you been putting two and two together young man? I can see from your expression that you have' she said.

Conrad took a deep breath and replied
'I really don't know what you are talking about. I do know, however, that at your age, you really shouldn't be playing Juliet'.

There was an icy silence in the room and then a long sigh as Michaela exhaled.
'You know Conrad, it's very hard to make it anywhere as a woman, but you do make a valid point. I was thinking of stepping back and taking a back seat. I've even made an offer to Penny Bright to buy out both the film and theatre company, she seems very keen'.

"The Daily Echo

Some tales are stranger than fiction. With two of its former associates now behind bars, the Princely Productions version of Shakespeare's Romeo and Juliet, starring industry unknowns Conrad Campbell and Beth Cleverley, transcends the drama that was the background to its creation. With stunning performances from its two young leads and charming cameo performances from its seasoned cast, notably Wendy-Jane Hughes and Laurence O'Halloran, this is a film not to be missed. Sure to be a favourite for years to come...."

"The London Gazette

....the cinematography and the unusually strong colour palette used by the make-up team heighten the feelings of emotion in this vibrant interpretation of a Shakespeare classic"

"Industry Insider

We will be watching the career of Michaela Prince in the future, following the success of Princely Productions debut film, Shakespeare's Romeo and Juliet. Our crystal ball predicts that this company is one to watch; we would advise investors to give Princely Productions serious consideration in the future..."

So that is how Conrad found himself sitting in an Art house cinema in Helmstone, staring up at a 20 foot high version of himself kissing a previously unknown actress; who was fresh out of Drama school.

He can now look forward to a lifetime of high-profile roles thanks to a very lucrative, and mutually beneficial, agreement with the now powerful producer Michaela Prince of Princely Productions. He is never going to end up on the cutting room floor again.

Demonic
by
Lizzie Jarrett

Demonic

Saturday 2nd February: 9.30 am
Days to expiry: 28 days

A letter dropped through the letterbox, but Isla thought nothing of it. Inside the envelope were words and sentences that might destroy one's sense of security and sense of self, but for now the letter is being ignored by its intended recipient. Isla is getting on with her chores as she always does; emptying the dishwasher and cleaning up after the cat. Blocking out the blandness of her life with an ever increasingly long list of mind-numbing activity.

Isla's twins, Scottie and Shona, are both beside themselves with excitement today; they have been invited to a birthday party at the local community centre.

Her husband has gone out for the day, lured out by a free round of golf and drinks at the bar afterwards. Isla is anticipating a lovely day of ….nothingness. Perhaps she would slob around and watch a film on the TV, the children weren't due to be back for hours.

Saturday 2nd February: 10.35 am

'Come along then you two, let's get you down to the party, we don't want to keep Jamie waiting.' Isla couldn't wait for her day of nothingness to commence.

The party didn't start for another twenty minutes and since it was only a five minute drive, her children were easily going to be the first guests.
'Hurry up then, that's right take the present with you.'

Isla had a strict rule, £5 only for a birthday present. It didn't matter that both her children were invited. She reasoned to herself that every other aspect of having twins was expensive, so why shouldn't she make savings where she could?

A quick drive led Isla and the twins straight to the local community centre, where a very harassed-looking mother was talking to a children's entertainer.

'See you later then' she said as she sprinted for the exit, before the "party" mum could make any unwanted conversation or, heaven forbid, ask her to stay….

Saturday 2nd February: 10.47 am

Five minutes later and she was back on her driveway, she stepped over the letter as she came in. It was in a black envelope, trimmed with red, slightly unusual…. Maybe it was advertising risqué underwear….? Without a second thought she picked the envelope up and ripped it open

"Dear Customer
Further to your Continuation of Life Policy, you will note that this policy is due to expire in one month's time. Our operative….."

Isla blinked and blinked again.
'Oh my God!' Her heart was beating faster and faster, a red pulse seemed to be throbbing in her ears; she felt quite sick. A multitude of feelings and emotions went through her mind; worry, anger, confusion, but mostly worry.

She looked down at the letter and the torn envelope, which were now down on the floor where she had dropped them. With trepidation she picked up the letter, she felt as though the contents might scald her. The ink, in which the letter was written, reminded her of something vaguely unpleasant and unsettling, like dried blood.

At the bottom of the page she could see a signature, it was a just a squiggle. But underneath she saw the printed name,

Dee Monique

Dee Monique, DeeMonique, Demonic!!! Isla laughed out loud. How could she have been so stupid? It was obviously a joke. Now she wished she had someone to share it with. She picked up the letter again and read it properly this time.

"D-Mon-Iq Insurance

Dear Customer
Further to your Continuation of Life Policy, you will note that this policy is due to expire in one month's time. Our operative will arrive to terminate you on, or about, the 2nd of March.

D-Mon-Iq would like to take this opportunity of thanking you for your custom over the years.

Yours faithfully

Dee Monique"

Someone had obviously gone to an immense amount of time and trouble to construct this letter. Who could it be? Was it malicious, or did she not fully appreciate a really good hoax? Her husband was always telling her that she had a "sense of humour deficit". At the bottom of the letter there was a phone number, maybe if she rang this she would find out that this was all a big joke?

Nervously she picked up the phone and tapped in the number. After a few rings she went straight through to a recorded message.

"Thank you for calling D-Mon-Iq Life Policies. All our operatives are out of the office at the current time attending to clients. Please call back at a later date...."

'Later date, later date'....Isla thought, she might be dead *at a later date*. This was not a joke any longer...and anyway what did *"attending to"* mean? She didn't like the sound of that.

Isla couldn't relax for the rest of the morning, the whole demented, demonic experience had unsettled her and the twins were distraught to see their mother turn up half an hour early to pick them up from their party.

Saturday 2nd February: 12.30

They were now rollerskating around the community centre hall playing some weird and extremely loud variant of It. There stood Isla her arms folded, tapping at her watch; the twins just kept on skating, round and round, faster and faster. Finally the "party mum" took pity on Isla.
'Here have a swig of this, my husband thinks I've got a thermos of tea. But I find that I need a little "extra help" to get through the afternoon.'
Isla swigged down a large cup of what turned out to be whiskey. Never her favourite, but under the circumstances she was very grateful.

Saturday 2nd February:13.30

Isla's husband, Doug, was having a fine old time that afternoon. His company, Timeless Insure, had recently gone into partnership with another company in the same field. The whole golf event was just one big "puff" to promote the partnership.

Having his second pint of Fosters at the bar, he was thrilled to be introduced to a determined-looking, little spitfire of a woman in her mid 20s.

'Doug, you must meet this young lady. She is one of the operatives from D-Mon-Iq'. Miles Allardyce, Doug's boss, is full of himself this afternoon. He really likes the feel and fit of this new company they are working with; it seems like they will stop at nothing to meet the individual client's specifications.

The "young lady" was, at first glance, small and round and certainly nothing to write home about. However at a second glance one could perceive that she had the most determined and aggressive expression which seemed to burn like a flame in her tigerish eyes. These yellow, brown eyes gleamed with energy and life like a predator; constantly on the lookout for weaker characters that she could pick off and destroy.

This determined little person now homed in on her latest prey. She took a deep breath, put on her most seductive smile, hitched up her skirt and opened her mouth.
'It's great to meet with you Doug. Boy, do I have an interesting proposition for you'.

***

Saturday 2nd February: 22.30

Doug turned up late that evening to find his wife cocooned in a purple blanket on the sofa. If he hadn't been so very late home he would have seen the massive dent in the side of Isla's car. A souvenir of her drunken, lurching ride back from the community centre. In some respects Isla had been quite lucky, she had nearly made it to the front driveway intact when a little red sports car had appeared from nowhere and had driven at collision course into the side of her car. The driver hadn't hung around to apologise and nobody had got a good look at the driver's face or the numberplate of the car.

Sunday 3rd February: 9.30 am
Days to expiry: 27 days

The next morning Isla was surprised to find that Doug had disappeared again for the day. A note on the pillow next to her read "early golf game". Isla was non-plussed, Doug had never so much played a game of Pitch and Putt until his golf game yesterday. Surely he must have seen the dent in her car as he left? She spent the whole day anticipating an angry phone call about the damage, but it never came.

Sunday 3rd February: 22.45

Doug was late home again that night, but Isla still made sure she told him about the letter she had received and the huge dent in the car. His response wasn't quite what she had expected.

'There you go again over-reacting, the letter is so obviously a hoax, whoever heard of something as ridiculous as a Life Continuation Policy....give me a break! I'm in the insurance game, you know, I would know if such a policy existed. As for the car, don't upset yourself darling, you just make sure you get it up to the garage first thing tomorrow and we will get it fixed.'

Isla is not sure whether she prefers her husband like this. Usually he'd have torn her off a strip about the dent in the car. Now he is *almost* helpful, what is wrong?

Monday 4th February:11 am
Days to expiry: 26 days

Driving back from the garage in the courtesy car, Isla notices there is a new addition to the close, someone who drives a small red sports car. It is parked on the drive of Isla's friend, Debbie Collins. It turns out that the car belongs to the Collins' new au-pair, just over from Newfoundland.

Like a 21st century compact version of Mary Poppins she has just turned up, seemingly out of nowhere.

'You know what Isla, she just turned up out of the blue, said that she had been told that we needed an

au-pair. I agreed on the spot, she's quite a little whirlwind, you know.'
Debbie, Isla's only friend on the close, was obviously thrilled with this sudden turn of events.

Isla was quite sure she would have liked an au-pair, although she wasn't altogether sure she whether she would have liked this one. Hadn't she seen that face before? She wished she could remember where. Come to that there was something familiar about the little red car too…

Any subsequent attempt to talk to Doug about the letter over the next few days and weeks was simply diverted, ignored or laughed at; he simply would not listen. One evening in desperation Isla picked up the telephone handset and rang the number of De-Mon-Iq herself…she then handed the phone to him.

'Listen to that!' she said in desperation.
'Listen to what? There's nothing there! You've been had, Isla! It was just a ridiculous joke and you fell for it.'
Her husband looked at her in a pitying way, as if she were a seven year old child.

Maybe Doug was right, after all…? She should write the whole thing off as a joke. What if she were simply depressed, perhaps she needed to see a doctor? Or maybe all she needed was a trip up town to cheer herself up?

Isla was definitely not one for shopping in the West end, she would have found everything too pricey for her tastes, but she did like the hustle and bustle of being in a crowd. She loved the anonymity of it all. That was settled, that was what she would do.

Friday 15th February: 10.55 am
Days to expiry: 15 days

The very next day she found herself hopping off the train at Victoria. The everyday military order of the railway station with everyone marching purposefully towards their individual goal made Isla feel that she was an essential part of some larger plan. She took a deep breath and then mustering up her courage, she took the steps down to the underground; the only part of the journey she knew she would not enjoy. Following the tube map she made her way to the correct platform for the train to Oxford Street.
Looking down at the track always made her feel dizzy, so she instinctively took a step backwards. Just as she did so she felt someone push her from behind and then she heard herself screaming, as she fell forwards towards the track.

She awoke to find herself kneeling right at the edge of the platform just as the train to Oxford Circus came thundering in.
'What happened?' she mumbled to a freckled Australian tourist who was offering her his arm. But nobody seemed to know a thing, people just wanted to get on with their busy day. Even the nice

young man who was helping her up had seen nothing and was simply just doing his good deed for the day by helping her get to her feet. She was left bruised and alone.

Friday 15th February: 11.30

Empty and deflated, Isla felt a return of the black feelings and helplessness that had been dogging her for the last week. She turned round, hobbled back on to the escalator and found herself returning home much earlier than she had anticipated; the mood for window shopping had completely deserted her.

Friday 15th February: 15.00

Needless to say she found herself arriving back at home in time to collect the children from school. She was surprised to see Debbie standing in the playground as well.
'Where's the au-pair then? I thought this was her job.' enquired Isla.
'Oh' replied her friend 'it's her day off. I think she went up to London…'

Friday 15th February: 18.00

Cooking the tea that evening Isla found herself looking idly at the calendar. It was the 15th of February, only just over 2 weeks to go…

How she got through those weeks, she did not know. Everyday was like living her life on the other side of double-glazed windows, people seemed remote and far away; she could hear herself talking, but it was if it were a different person. Her every action required immense effort, from getting dressed in the morning to putting one foot in front of the other. It was like trying to wade through liquid toffee.

Friday 1st March 07.30 am
Days to expiry: 1 day

Finally, like a huge and ominous tombstone casting a black shadow over the following day, the first of March arrived.

Friday 1st March: 15.00

In the afternoon Isla went to collect the children from school and was surprised to find that they had already left with someone else.
'Who was it?' Isla demanded of the newly-qualified, and suddenly terrified, teacher who stood in front of her.
'It was the Collins' children's au-pair. She said she had been asked to pick your children up as well.'
"Bloody teacher, she had no right to let the children go." Isla fumed to herself, as she found herself powering purposely up the road towards her friend's house.

Friday 1st March:15.30

By the time she arrived at the front door there was practically steam issuing from both ears.
'Where are my children?' she found herself demanding of Debbie.
'They're here with me. Why don't you let them spend the night here? Linzi picked them all up from school. We both thought you'd like a treat. Linzi said you'd been looking so tired recently….Go home, have an early night. I'll look after the children, it's Linzi's night off. She said she had a little job to do for a friend.'

Friday 1st March: 22.00

Becalmed and bewildered, by the time Isla collapsed into bed alongside her husband she no longer cared what the date on the calendar said. She would just drink her Horlicks and everything would be okay in the morning. She was asleep before her head hit the pillow.

Saturday 2nd March 9.30 am
Policy expired

She woke on the 2nd of March and looked down at her hand and was surprised to see that she could see straight through it. She looked again up and down her body and noted that she could see the duvet underneath her. As she turned her head to look at her husband, she saw him turn dreamy-eyed and smiling towards a young woman who had just entered the room.

It was that bloody au-pair from over the road. Isla realised too late where she had seen those distinctive eyes before, when they had been bearing down on her from behind the wheel of a little red sports car. Her husband had renewed a policy alright, it was just that it wasn't the one with his wife's name on it.

'I'll just go and bleach out this cup of Horlicks, shall I? You go and get my car and pull it onto the drive.' The girl laughed triumphantly, as she threw her car keys towards Isla's husband.

The Friendly Society of Witches
by
Lizzie Jarrett

1.

Geri Oliver had never had any money worries in her life, or indeed any worries at all. So it was a great shock to her to find that when her husband of thirty years unexpectedly left her for another woman, not only was she suddenly penniless, but that she also had lots of new worries and, surprisingly to her, very few real friends at all.

Her husband, Clive had always insisted that Geri had no need to work when they first got married and, despite the fact that she had met him at university and had graduated with a good degree, she had gladly consented to this arrangement. She happily bore him two children, a boy and a girl, and they enjoyed many blissful years together as an ideal family. They holidayed in the Caribbean, went to the tennis club together and had many, many pleasant dinner parties with their lovely friends.

But now, due to the intervention of a third party, Geri was a fifty-four year old, newly single woman with no bank account of her own. With no income she most certainly wouldn't be holidaying in the Caribbean anytime soon.

Dear Mrs. Oliver

Account name: Mr. C.J. and Mrs. G. E. Oliver
Account number: XXXXXXXXX

It has come to our attention that the above account has been emptied of funds, please do not continue to present your bank card. This bank does not facilitate an overdraft facility.

To avoid unpleasantness we suggest you approach another financial body that may wish to do business with you.

Yours faithfully

L.J. Smythe

Geri's membership of the tennis club was no longer valid and somebody else was going to dinner parties with her husband at the houses of people, she had discovered, who were most definitely no longer her friends.

Dear Madam

Please do not continue to use our past friendship as proof of a valid and current membership of the Billingsborough Tennis Club.

Whilst you were indeed fortunate to have enjoyed membership of such a prestigious institution, I am firmly of the belief that it is now time for you to move on to pastures new. I would remind you that membership is also conditional on having a provable income of over £50,000 pa.

Our four year waiting list means that your membership is now null and void and your place has been taken by a new member.

Yours faithfully

H.O. Oswestry-Mills

What to do? What to do? What to do? For the first few months she had tried to carry on as before, but the complete lack of money soon made her day-to-day life totally impossible. Her credit cards had all been cancelled and she was soon reduced to accepting hand-outs from her children, Jasmine and Richard.
'Mum, why don't you come and stay with me?' said her daughter. This suggestion was finally very gratefully, and graciously, accepted.

2.

Jasmine lived alone in the village of Wycheswode. She worked as a farrier, which had been a massive disappointment to her mother and father at the time. But now Jasmine was in the enviable position of being able to thwart expectations; since business was doing very well and she was the owner of a very nice cottage with an extremely convenient spare room.

Geri and Clive's son, Richard, lived in Dubai, and whilst he was sympathetic to his mother, there was not very much he could do for her, other than send her financial aid in this time of direst need.

After several weeks filling her days walking Jasmine's dog and getting to know the local surroundings a small ad in the local chemist's window caught her eye:

Have you got time on your hands?
Help needed, apply within.

Before marriage intervened Geri had, at least, managed to acquire a degree in Pharmacy. How was Mr. Foot, the chemist, going to turn down such a find? So from having not worked in over twenty-five years Geri suddenly found that she had a job to go to. She found she enjoyed the mundanity of getting up every day, wearing her uniform and being the friendly face of Foots the Chemist.

Although she was not the dispensing chemist, her mature years and welcoming manner meant that customers would assume that she had expert knowledge and confide in her the most intimate of medical details. She could soon identify particular groups of customers. There were the teenage depressives, for example; pale and undernourished, turning their anger in on themselves and suppressing this rage with anti-depressants. Geri worried about these customers the most and wished there was some other way they could be helped, other than taking tablets. There were of course, the middle-aged depressives and the old-age depressives too.

Then there were the women of a certain age who had decided that their body's biological clock was not going to determine how they felt and what they could achieve. They signed on the dotted line for their HRT prescriptions and were out of the door before you could say "menopause". Geri had no real experience of the menopause, however she did have enough other problems to contend with at the moment; so maybe she wouldn't even have noticed the symptoms.

Other patients were just so unfortunate that nothing ever went well for them. Overburdened low wage families with chronically ill children for whom the better prescription would be *six months free food shopping*, but instead they had to stand in line with everyone else to receive the latest pharmaceutical miracle, or sometimes just a bunch of sugar pills. For the first time in a while Geri started to count her blessings and forget about her husband.

3.

Clive Oliver was not missing his wife at all; he had a new distraction, his girlfriend, Sophia. This young lady had, up until very recently, been Clive's intern at his architectural practice in London. Clive enjoyed the glamour of having this beautiful young thing on his arm; he loved taking her out to dinner and to the tennis club and very soon they were going on a lovely Caribbean holiday together.

Geri was starting to enjoy her village life routine and felt herself to be a respected local character. The only thing she was missing now was a group of friends. She decided to take matters into her own hands and advertise on the noticeboard outside the village hall. Geri felt that in the light of recent events, it had to be a women only group. She took her time before penning an appropriately worded advert. Then, very carefully, she highlighted the advert in purple marker pen; picking out the first letter of each line. She then waited eagerly for Friday to arrive to see what would transpire.

T*urn up at the Village*
H*all*
E*very Friday at 7pm for*

C*akes and Conversation*
R*eadings*
A*rt Appreciation*
F*riendship*
T*ime Together*
(Please note this is a women only group)

The noticeboard soon attracted some interest. A tall thin lady adorned in purple and the proud possessor of many a capacious and colourful shawl, noted down the details in a small notepad that she kept in her purple macrame handbag. Lesley Leigh was a local alternative therapist, the advert seemed to speak to her. This was exactly what she needed.

A yellow-faced girl of seventeen, with rather unfortunately dyed hair tapped the details down on to her phone. Her hair, which was naturally chestnut brown, had been dyed to such an inky-blackness that the edge of her face seemed almost green, as the hair met her sallow skin. Karys Hughes often felt alone and isolated because of her outlandish appearance and her strange interests. But the postcard on the noticeboard seemed to confirm to her that she was not alone.

Mary Downs worked at the local Bizzy Shopper and Friday was her only night off. She could do with some lady friends or indeed any social life at all, outside of the shop. Mary didn't know why, but her very appearance and her family connections seemed to put people off. But Geri's notice seemed to confirm to Mary that somebody out there was willing to accept her for what she was.

The very last person to view the postcard was on her way back home from the hairdressers, having just had her hair dyed a very vivid shade of pink. You would have thought that she would not want to stand about in the drizzle, but Geri's postcard seemed to hold some special attraction for her. She took out her phone and snapped a photo. She would *definitely* be there on Friday.

Friday came and Geri returned home to the cottage to find her daughter home in advance of her.
'Mum…' she said
'Yes dear'
'You know the postcard you put up on the noticeboard?'

'Yes dear, I do'
'Had you ever thought that you might get more than you bargained for?'
'What do you mean dear?' said Geri, as she absent-mindedly stared at the wonky clock on the kitchen wall.
'Don't worry mum, it's just me imagining things… but just remember you do live in Wycheswode now…'

Geri was just about to set foot outside the front door when Jasmine's defences broke down and she heard her daughter say. 'Mum, I don't know how to tell you this, but dad has just sent me some pictures of him and "that girl" on holiday at "Le Paradis" resort, the one we always went to. What a bastard!'
Without turning back to face Jasmine, Geri set off at top speed towards the village hall
with those inflammatory words ringing in her ears.

4.

Since she was the group instigator and organiser Geri honestly expected to be the first one to arrive, but was surprised to be greeted by a red-faced woman of about thirty, sporting bright pink hair.
'Hi there, my name's Katherine Crichton, Kat for short. I'm looking forward to getting up to some mischief tonight!'
Geri hoped that she could supply the "mischief" that Kat was looking for. She had some very grave

doubts though, after all it was only meant to be a comfy cake and friendship group…

Within a very short space of time they were joined by a tall thin woman, dressed in purple who was called Lesley and a strange-looking teenager clad in goth clothing, who said her name was Karys. Geri thought she recognised Karys; it was probably from the chemist's.

Just as they were finishing their "how do you dos" the door opened and a small, dumpy lady, still wearing a Bizzy Shopper uniform, came in.
'Oh God, not her…' Geri heard Kat mutter.
'You're very welcome,' said Geri to the newcomer, in a rather moralistic and "headmistressy" tone, after all surely everyone should be made welcome.
'I've brought cake,' the little lady said.
'So have I' said Kat 'it's my own special recipe.'
'Well, I've brought some lovely herbal tea,' said the tall purple-clad lady.

As soon as the tea and the cakes were divvied out, Geri made a short speech welcoming them all as women who have suffered and talked about the virtues of living life without men. The ladies all seemed very appreciative of that. Then, just before the cakes were consumed, Kat said something which Geri did not understand, it was along the lines of "we can get down to the serious business next week", but since the other ladies all applauded her, Geri did not bother to ask what the serious business might be.

Kat's "special ingredient" brownies

Ingredients:

185g butter (stir in 7g special ingredient)
185g dark chocolate
50g milk chocolate/white chocolate
85g flour
40g cocoa powder
3 large eggs
275g golden caster sugar

- *Put dark chocolate, "special ingredient" and butter in a glass bowl and then melt slowly using "bain marie" method.*
- *Sieve flour and cocoa together.*
- *Mix the eggs together with the sugar.*
- *Pour the melted chocolate mix over the whipped eggs and sugar.*
- *Add in the sieved cocoa and flour and then add chunks of unused chocolate.*
- *Pour mixture into a foil baking tray.*
- *Cook at 160 deg (fan oven) for 25 minutes.*
- *Allow to cool.*
- *Cut into brownie sized bites.*
- *Eat and enjoy that "special taste".*

After this the evening seemed to fly by, as if by magic. Geri was unsure, but she may have fallen asleep for a moment, because the next thing she knew Mary Downs was patting her on the shoulder and handing her an envelope.

'Kat says you'll know what to do with this.' Mary said.
'Okay then.' Geri smiled obligingly back at Mary, wished her goodnight and made her way home.

5.

On waking the next morning Jasmine got something of a shock when she went downstairs and saw her mother's bedroom door still closed. She opened the door to find her mother still fast asleep. It was 8.30 in the morning and she was due on duty at the chemists in half an hour.

With a large dose of coffee inside her, Geri arrived late at work rather befuddled and dishevelled. Mr. Foot was quite put out, seeing her arrive in such an "unfragrant" state; it rather dented his aspirations towards this still attractive, and available, lady of a certain age.

Geri, for her part, wondered how she managed to get through the morning. She certainly had no recollection of arriving home last night and when Jasmine had awoken her she had been lying face down on her pillow, with a stream of dribble glued to her chin.

The Legend of Wycheswode and the Wycheswode Witch

The clue is in the name, wyches = witches
wode = wood. Centuries ago much of England was heavily wooded, Sussex held onto its woods and forests for longer

than many counties, it also held onto its witches. Sussex was the last county to convert to Christianity from the old Pagan beliefs. The county has always been relatively tolerant of outsiders and has never burned a witch, although it did once allow the burning of Protestants in Westwick High Street.....

The Wycheswode Witch, Sarah Downs, known locally as Silly Sarah, was famous for her benevolence and also the relative ineffectiveness of her magic. It is believed that her family have continued to make Wycheswode their home, although whether they are better witches is unknown...

Excerpt from Weird Sussex, a compilation of strange and bizarre stories from across the county compiled by Ray Richardson, available at selected booksellers.

In actual fact "wyches" does not mean witches, it means "natural springs", but for the purposes of selling a book Ray Richardson's publishers had decided to leave things as they were. If it meant the association with witchcraft would sell one more book, then they would leave the quote in.

That evening Jasmine decided that it was time for a serious chat with her mother.
'Mum, I never thought I would be having this conversation, but what did you get up to last night?'
'What do you mean dear?'
'Well, mum. You arrived home really late last night, you then sat in the lounge eating biscuits and

laughing at the telly until about half past one in the morning. Were you drunk?'
'No dear, we just had tea and cake'
'Wow! You'll be telling me next they were special recipe brownies!'
'Yes dear, they were!'
'That explains it...and what were the names of these other ladies?' queried Jasmine, sounding for all the world like the mother not the daughter.
Geri thought for a while....
'I can't quite remember, I do know that the funny little lady from the Bizzy Shopper was there.'
'Mum! Everybody in the village says she's a witch. Apparently her family has lived here for centuries, they are the reason the village is called Wycheswode'.
'Oh, I really don't think so dear....anyway it wasn't her who gave me the tea or the brownies'.
Jasmine decided to make her point now and then be done with it.
'Mum, I've got to tell you now. The way you wrote your advert was just asking for weirdos! You wrote "Women only" for a start. Then the way you highlighted your advert, you do realise you wrote "THE CRAFT" and we all know that stands for...'

6.

As a matter of fact, Geri was one of the few people in the western world who didn't know what that meant and I'm not sure if she really understands now. The other ladies, however, all knew exactly what it meant. They all had their strange and different reasons and agendas for attending. Lesley Leigh really did wish to expand her horizons to include not only alternative therapy, but also witchcraft; she felt it might be her true calling.

Karys felt that witches might be the only people that could truly understand her. Coincidentally Karys had also woken very late and strangely confused on the Saturday morning, thanks to Lesley's tea and Kat's brownies. Her mother was rather concerned, not amused and definitely not very understanding.

Kat felt that only witchcraft could settle a personal score. Her girlfriend, Evie, with whom she had been on the verge of buying a flat, had left her for another woman. Kat was in a state of high emotional distress. It was she who after the tea and brownies had introduced the idea of the "Do me a favour" game.

The minute that Geri had bitten into Kat's homemade brownies, the secret ingredient had triggered an emotional tidal wave against her husband.
'Who does he think he is? Leaving me for his young tart. I've got no money, no house and no friends. I wish someone would teach him a lesson.'
All of these pent up words and feelings came tumbling out of Geri's mouth.

That was all the invitation that Kat had needed. She quickly produced from her bag a pack of notelets and envelopes. All the ladies seemed willing, they simply wrote down their most intimate and immediate wish and then they swapped envelopes. Kat had one in her possession that read *"Teach him a lesson"*. Karys had one from Lesley that read *"Magic up a friend for my daughter"*. Lesley had one from Karys that said *"Show me I am not alone"* and Geri had an unopened envelope at the bottom of her handbag with God knows what written inside.

Mary had nothing, because she had spent the evening just listening in, as usual, and then she had stayed late to wash and wipe up. It's a good job she did so, because the Women's Institute were due in the hall the very next morning and what they would have made of the smell of the special tea and the special ingredient brownie crumbs….well, we will never know.

The funny thing was, Mary was the only one in the room who actually *was* a witch. A bona-fide, hereditary living relative of Sarah Downs *and* a far more effective witch. But, as with her great-great-great-great-great-great grandmother, Mary could not cast a spell that would affect her in any way, either negatively or positively. Since if she could cast a spell for herself she would most definitely not be working in the Bizzy Shopper. She found herself ostracised and mocked by the local community, but if just one of them had ever stopped to ask her she would have been delighted to cast a spell. She would have done anything for the simple friendship of another living soul; that was her motivation for attending Geri's meeting.

7.

Geri herself spent the next few days trying to work her way back into Mr. Foot's good books. She was early every day, she was smartly turned out and friendly to everyone. Things took a change for the peculiar when, on returning to her till on Wednesday lunchtime, she was alarmed to find a small notelet placed on top personally addressed to her. Inside in vibrant pink handwriting it said "*The Deed is Done!*". It was only when Geri and Jasmine received a midnight phone call from St. Thomas' hospital that the words on the card truly made sense.

Clive Oliver was dangerously ill, the hospital suspected that he had been poisoned and advised his next-of-kin to attend immediately. Despite her suppressed feelings, and whatever she might have said after a special recipe brownie or two, Geri was in deep shock. Very early on Thursday morning the two women found themselves in St. Thomas' hospital at Clive's bedside, opposite a very distraught Sophia.

'I bet you were just waiting for something like this to happen, weren't you? You might even have poisoned him yourself!' screamed the irate girlfriend.

'And just how would my mother have done that?' asked Jasmine incredulously.

'You old witch! You're just lucky he's going to pull through. You could have been facing trial for murder!' Sophia continued.

Crazy Catering

Let us give your event that Crazy edge with our themed event catering. In the past year we have staged events for many firms in the city. We can cater from A-Z. From Accountants and Architects to Zen Masters and Zoo-keepers, we produce cakes, confectionery and sugar craft to match your theme. You won't regret giving Crazy Catering a call…

What Sophia didn't know was that her own infantile obsession with cakes and sugar meant that she had been a key player in Clive's downfall. She had hired Crazy Catering on Monday that week after a surprise visit from one of their representatives, a powerhouse of a woman with very bright pink hair. The woman had persuaded Sophia that Crazy Catering could deliver a surprise architecture-themed cake. A mini-cake at the top of the main cake was reserved especially for Clive; he had eaten it all in one go, not a crumb was left.

Kat was certainly not one to hatch a plan without taking precautions. All mixing bowls used and any other incriminating cake kitchenalia had now been disposed of in various recycling bins across the capital.

Geri stared into space all the way home.
'How ridiculous…fancy thinking you had anything to do with it,' said Jasmine.
'Yes, fancy…' murmured Geri remembering, with a chill, the cryptic message she had found at work, "The Deed is Done!". 'Who could have done such a thing?'
'Mum' said Jasmine 'did you notice that Sophia is pregnant?'

8.

Friday had arrived once more. Lesley and Karys had easily been able to "cast a spell" and create a friend for Lesley's miserable, anorexic daughter. That friend was Karys. In return Lesley's daughter, Cassandra, fitted the bill to be Karys' new best friend. Mary was once again handing out some cakes, luckily they were from the Bizzy Shopper and not from Kat's kitchen, they had just passed their sell-by date.

Geri was on her guard as she arrived that evening.
'I've had a funny old week,' she said out loud.
'Sorry things didn't go as planned, shall I give it another go?' said Kat
Geri felt herself take a sharp intake of breath before she said 'Sorry, I don't know what you're talking about.'

'Of course you don't…but don't forget Geri, a deal's a deal…' added Kat, as she bit into one of the stale cakes.

It was a very fraught and stone-cold sober Geri who, that evening, fished to the bottom of her very large leather handbag and pulled out an unopened envelope. The writing inside the card was strangely familiar. It read *"She's allergic to Penicillin, one wrongly labelled prescription should do it!"* Accompanying this card was a dog-eared photo of an attractive-looking girl of twenty-five or so, who had vivid pink hair.

'Oh…my…God!' screamed Geri, 'what have I got myself mixed up in?'. Wandering along the landing, she found herself tapping on her daughter's bedroom door.
'Jazz, Jazz…wake up!'
'Come in mum, how can I help you?' said her daughter smiling kindly back at her.
'Look at this!', said Geri, holding out the now tear-stained notelet in her hand.
'Mum, leave it to me. I will sort it out. Now go to bed, you've got to go to work in the morning, remember?'

Visitors to the Wycheswode Bizzy Shopper that Saturday would have been surprised to find it being staffed by two goth-looking teenagers. Whilst any unexpected drop-ins to the Wycheswode forge were met by a dramatically clad lady, all in purple, who informed them: 'The lady farrier is away from her forge at the moment. If you would like to stay for a cup of tea or a tarot reading, I can take your details and Jasmine will return shortly.'

9.

The local pub was an unlikely meeting place for a dowdy little shop assistant and a vibrant lady farrier. However they found, after a few awkward moments, that they got on surprisingly well. After Jasmine had enquired whether Mary could deal with her mother's outstanding favour for Kat, she may then have asked Mary if she liked Prosecco. Mary found that she did indeed like Prosecco.

That night at eleven pm, Kat was awoken from her sleep by a phone call from the local A & E.
'We've got a very upset young lady here by the name of Evie, she's broken her leg. She says you're the only family she's got. Will you come and pick her up?' said a woman's voice at the other end of the line.
Kat thought for a moment, then said 'Of course I will, I'll be there as soon as I can.'
Driving her little pink car to the hospital, she mused to herself "It's a good job Geri didn't go through with the deal'.
But of course she did. After all Kat didn't manage to actually kill off Clive so therefore Geri's side of the deal meant all she had to do was inconvenience Evie.

Mary was just glad to help. She's got at least four new friends now *and* she has got Saturday girls to call on whenever she doesn't want to be in the shop. She has also continued with her appreciation of Prosecco.

Kat and Evie are back together and, just as soon as Evie's leg is healed, they will pursue their plan of buying a home together.

Jasmine has got the occasional use of a tall glamorous receptionist and Geri's son, Richard, doesn't have to send any more emergency cash supplies to Wycheswode. Geri is continuing to keep a very careful eye on any prescriptions that leave Wycheswode chemists, you can never be too careful…

The only people that aren't happy are Clive and Sophia; apparently she's expecting octuplets. How the ultrasonographer could have missed the other seven foetuses nobody will ever know. The poor woman swears they weren't there a week ago. But Jasmine and Mary wouldn't know anything about that, would they? After all, who can remember what was said after the fourth glass of Prosecco?

In the kitchen of a small unassuming cottage, that the Downs family has made their home for the last four hundred years, Mary Downs is standing on a step-ladder. She is returning a very special and treasured family book back to its hiding place; it is now stowed safely inside a large biscuit tin. She doesn't get the book down very often, but she needed help with a couple of "recipes". On the pages inside Mary's dirty fingerprints, on pages 54 and 97, betray the last recipes used.

p.54
Fertility curse: to cause a woman to gain more children in her womb.
*For each extra child desired, add one extra egg.
p.97
Lover come back to me: to cause illness or broken bone and make your lover dependent on you.

*worked well, would definitely try this one again.

The Ring of Unluck
by
Lizzie Jarrett

1.

Archaeological dig - excavations are due to take place of the Saxon graveyard at St. Swithun's church in Godmanshurst, Wessex. This church and the settlement nearby are thought to have been abandoned since the late Tudor times; due to a plague outbreak in the 1500s.
No experience necessary, just a keen interest in British heritage. Phone Bramblehurst - 622594 for further details.

Amanda Ellis was waiting for her daughter, Emma, to have her braces removed, when an advert in a local magazine caught her eye. She had always wondered what it would be like to go an archaeological dig. Her only experience had been third hand, like most people, through watching Indiana Jones movies; hardly a reliable source of information. She saw herself digging up some fascinating gold artefact and being interviewed on local TV, when news of her find had spread further afield.

As Emma emerged from the treatment room, smiling her newly straightened and brace-free smile from ear to ear, Amanda tore out the notice from the magazine and stuffed it into her handbag.

The piece of paper remained screwed up in the depths of her handbag and would have stayed forgotten, but for a chance remark from Emma later on that week.

'Sarah Fletcher's mum came in to school today and gave a talk about a course she is doing. She's studying to be an archaeologist....'

Amanda snorted and tried not to choke on her breakfast cereal. The very idea, *that* woman an archaeologist, whatever next!

'Sarah and her family are going to Egypt in the holidays, whilst her mum is on a dig....She doesn't look like an archaeologist, does she mum? She's ever so glamorous. I love her clothes, I wonder where she shops?'

Amanda sniffed again, to try and cover up the derisive snort she had made earlier. She had always loathed Sarah Fletcher's mum, Becky. Whatever that woman touched seemed to turn to gold. Mrs. Fletcher worked as an air hostess and her husband worked in the Futures market, whatever that was? She was also a school governor, who always managed to be immaculately clad even when standing at the school gates. At the end of the school day Mrs. Fletcher could often be found dispensing words of wisdom to other mothers, whom she had decided needed her good counsel. Next to Mrs. Fletcher, Amanda felt cross, inadequate and distinctly unglamorous. Amanda wasn't to know that the woman was an alcoholic, an awful mother and was over her limit on all her credit cards, much to the irritation of her overworked husband.

2.

At the very next opportunity Amanda was on the phone to the number shown on the advert. The lady at the other end of the line joked away.
'As long as you're prepared to sleep in the crypt, that's okay. Bring your walking boots and something to kneel on and, most importantly, bring waterproof clothing.'
What a card, thought Amanda, "Sleep in the crypt!". What a sense of humour that woman must have, I bet she tried that joke on everyone.

There has been speculation for years as to the reason for the desertion of St. Swithun's church and the nearby village of Godmanshurst in the 1600s. It is commonly assumed that the villagers of Godmanshurst were stricken by the plague in late Tudor times, since this once thriving village seemed to disappear from the history books at around about this time. In the town of nearby Bramblehurst residents speak of a curse, although nobody was able to be specific about the nature of the curse or the reasons for a curse being issued...

Wessex villages, past and present by John Beaconsfield, available at all good booksellers.

So it was with some dismay that within minutes of arriving at St. Swithun's church, outside Bramblehurst in Wessex, Amanda was shown to the crypt; where a group of grungy and weather-beaten archaeology students had deposited their sleeping bags. Under the circumstances, Amanda thought nothing of telling a huge lie.

'Oh well, my old friend, John Smith, lives just nearby. I'll be staying with him since he has so kindly offered.'
A quick drive back into the nearest market town and she had soon found a room at a local hotel.

The digging itself was a very tedious matter; on your knees surrounded by piles of oozing clay trying to take an interest in the burial position of the poor unfortunate individual whose grave they might be excavating today. Amanda took a deep breath and thought once again of the Brownie points she would be gaining from her daughter.

The clothes she had purchased especially to wear on the dig were soon splattered with mud like a low-rent Jackson Pollock painting rendered solely in brown. Whilst her previously unused wellington boots, gaily decorated with yellow and red tulips, were soon inelegantly caked in fifty shades of clay.

On the first and second days she managed to get away at the end of digging without socialising too much with these archaeology types. She had excused herself by creating imaginary friends and relatives who had come down to Bramblehurst just to see her.

On the fifth day the excuses were, even to Amanda, starting to sound a tad manufactured. So she found herself sitting in the crypt of St. Swithun's; as Dr. Mallory, the archaeologist leading the dig, served out a generous helping of beef stew.

This was all washed down with snakebite; that lethal beer and cider mix. As the evening wore on and more and more snakebite was imbibed, the atmosphere got more and more rowdy. Amanda judged it was probably a safe time to beat a retreat.

Weaving her way slightly unsteadily out of the crypt, the sole of her boots crunched against something small and sharp. She leant down and yanked it out of the rubber sole and plopped it into her pocket. Once safely back inside her BMW she meandered her way drunkenly back along the country roads to her hotel.

3.

Waking next morning to another rain-soaked day in Wessex, Amanda helped herself to a second croissant and some fruit salad from the breakfast bar. She felt she really and truly had "enjoyed" enough of the archaeological life and didn't think that, in good faith, she could fake another day of enthusiasm for the long-dead inhabitants of this soggy corner of Wessex. With her mind made up to leave that very day, she returned to her room to pack.

With everything crammed back into her neat little suitcase, she picked up the mud-spattered raincoat that she had been wearing all week; that had better go home with her as well. She rolled it up tight into a ball, but as she forced it down into the case she felt something hard in the pocket. Taking the jacket by the hem, she shook it violently hoping to dislodge the contents. All that emerged was a Murray mint, still in its wrapper and two or three tissues. She knew that there was still something stuck in the pocket. Feeling inside she found that a hole had been torn and that whatever it was had got stuck inside the lining. This piqued her interest, using a complimentary hotel pen she rifled away inside the lining, but still the item would not dislodge itself.

'Well, I'm not going to wear this again, so what the hell!' she said and taking out her nail scissors she cut a large hole out of the lining. The "whatever it was" shot out and landed on the carpet in front of her. As it span around a shard of light entering the window illuminated the gold and precious stones it contained.

4.

Amanda's family were surprised to find their mother arrive home a good week earlier than they had anticipated. Emma had organised a sleepover and she and her friend, Georgia, were busy eating popcorn upstairs. Her husband, Andrew, who was enjoying a night in, had just ordered a Mega Meal Deal from the local Pizza house.
'What brings you home so early?' said Andrew, somewhat ungallantly.
'Does this mean Georgia has to go home early?' asked her daughter, remembering her mum's tough rules on sleepovers; they were completely off-limits.

Amanda's mind was elsewhere. Feigning deafness and indifference, she bunged her clothes in the quick wash cycle and headed off upstairs.

The minute she got up to her room she is able to look at the "whatever it was"; which she was now wearing on the ring finger of her right hand.

The ring is a beauty to behold. An exquisite gold band and mounted in the centre is a large opal surrounded by diamonds. She is in two minds what to tell her family. Should she go for glory and show off her find or should she hide it away? If she shows off the ring she will have a lot of questions to answer. Upon consideration she couldn't possibly let anyone know about the find. Best keep quiet and hope no-one asks any awkward questions.

Over the next few weeks her family started to notice a distinct change in her behaviour. From being rather proper and uptight she seemed to have progressed to…well, it was hard to describe; definitely secretive and yet rather pleased with herself.

To her husband it could mean only one thing; she must have met another man. Though in some ways they had outgrown each other, Andrew did not want to be the one who was being discarded. Her daughter, Emma, couldn't work it out at all. She knew her mum was supposed to have been on an archaeological dig, so what had she found? Why didn't she want to talk about it, like Sarah's mum did? How disappointed she was in her mother, once again.

Amanda herself simply felt trapped. She sensed that the ring must be worth something, but at the same time if she said anything she would be immediately unmasked as a thief. Her thoughts went round and round in circles: what should she do with the ring?
Events rather overtook her one evening, when she thought that she was alone. She had taken the ring out of its hiding place and tried it on. It was beautiful; the gold band caught the light, the diamonds sparkled and spectacular hues of purples, pinks, yellows and greens were reflected from the opal centre.

Yet she was not alone, she was being watched and to her husband the ring's very existence was proof positive of another man's involvement.
'Who is he? What's his name?' he demanded.
'There's no-one…' Amanda protested.
'Well, how do you explain that ring then?' Andrew continued.
'I found it, I swear I did…' said Amanda
'Oh really, that is so childish, surely you could have come up with a better lie than that?'. Andrew couldn't believe what she was saying.
'It's true!' she continued.

'If you found it then give it to me, let me look at it!' Andrew held out his hand; for her to surrender it to him.

'No, it's mine, I found it, you can't have it!' Amanda felt distraught at the idea of letting the ring out of her possession.

'Take it then and go!', and with that Andrew bundled her down the stairs, throwing her clothes and her car keys after her.

The Legend of the Ring of Unluck

Legend has it that in Tudor times a local girl, named Leonore, was promised in marriage to the rich and elderly Lord Bertram of Bramblehurst. A beautiful ring was given to the maiden, as a token of the impending nuptials. The ring was of such beauty; fashioned out of gold with a large opal at its very centre surrounded by exquisitely cut diamonds. However, the young lady's head was turned by the local blacksmith, a strapping and handsome youth who, beside her intended husband, seemed like a young Adonis.

The maiden and the blacksmith soon consummated their love. The lady, who was now a maiden no more, grew too bold and flaunted her new love in front of her friends. News of this affair reached her intended, but rather than have her put in the stocks, he named her as a witch and asked for the highest penalty.

It was whilst she burned at the stake that the fair Leonore threw the ring with such force at the stained glass window of the church that a pane of glass was smashed. As the ring was thrown onlookers heard her say, "A curse on this village, a curse on all men, a curse on this ring!".

The whereabouts of the ring are unknown, but should you be so unlucky as to find it, please hand it on to the Bishop of Wessex who will know what to do.

Excerpt from Wessex legends by Meredith Mallory published by Witan Press, available at selected bookshops.

5.

Back at St. Swithun's church Dr. Mallory and his team have been far too busy to notice Amanda's absence from the dig. From the very first day that she was absent the dig has had a renaissance, all sorts of paraphenalia and grave goods have been turning up; it's as if the earth has tired of holding on to the past. Only this morning Dr. Mallory has been able to get another six months funding for the dig and there is talk of a visit from the local television station.
'Well done Graham' says Dr. Mallory's wife, Meredith, 'If the dig continues on like this, you might get your own TV special on the History channel'.
Graham Mallory just can't believe his luck, this dig hadn't promised much, but almost overnight it has turned into a treasure hoard.

Many miles away, in a less than prestigious B & B on the wrong side of town, a tired and frustrated woman sits at the end of her bed. She is staring at the beautiful ring on her finger: yet she knows deep down inside that there is a connection between the ring and her current miserable circumstances. Amanda has been living in this rather squalid little room for three weeks now; she looks like a condemned woman, demented and on the edge of reason.

'Bloody thing, what am I supposed to do with you?' she exclaims in desperation. The opal and the diamonds that surround it sparkle in the flickering light given off by the TV screen. She clenches her hand round its loveliness and then bangs her head with her fists.

M & W Services

Money Worries? Let us help you.

Gold bought and sold
Pawnbroking
Cheques cashed

55 Tollgate Square, Westgate
Open Monday-Saturday 9-5.30

Through the door of M & W Services comes a worried and lonely figure. Amanda Ellis, wretched and driven to desperation, pushes forward her clenched fist, nestled inside is the most exquisite piece of jewellery that Maurice White, the owner, has ever seen.

'I'll give you a £100 for it,' he says, sensing the woman's desperation.

Amanda sighs, she knows in her heart that it is worth far more than that, but she has lost so much of her self-esteem over the last few weeks that she hasn't got the strength to argue. She stuffs the money into her purse and beats a retreat, even freeing herself from the ring for one minute has already lightened the load she feels she is carrying.

Maurice is bloody pleased with himself. That ring will fly off the shelf, he knows it. He should easily be able to double his profit.

But the weeks go by and the ring does not move. Its very presence in the shop seems to have marked out a red line on the floor of the shop that says "DO NOT CROSS". Custom becomes so bad, it's as if people are boycotting the shop. Give Maurice a standard engagement ring, a few diamonds on a gold band and it will dance out of the shop within days, leaving him with a healthy mark-up. But this ring, people just don't want to know, in fact some people seem positively frightened by it.

6.

Vai jūs runājat labā angļu valodā? Ir daudz iespēju strādāt strādājošiem. E-pasts šodien un mēs atradīsim jums darbu, lai dotos. Mēs piedāvājam konkurētspējīgas cenas. Augsts darbinieku skaits darbā aprūpes nozarē, lauksaimniecībā un arī tūrisma nozarē.
Ko tu gaidi?

Do you speak good English? There are lots of opportunities for hard-working people. Email us today and we will find you a job to go to. We offer competitive rates. High rates of recruitment in the Care sector, Farming and also in the Tourism sector.
What are you waiting for?

dmitrijs@goodjobsinuk.lv.en

Emils Balodis and his girlfriend, Mareka, have come to Britain from Latvia with high hopes. They are here to work hard, to earn money to send home to their extended family. Mareka packs in-flight meals on the industrial estate, while Emils has a job delivering parcels. When they left Latvia these were not the jobs they were thinking of, but at least they are together and the money is better here than what they could earn back home.

Emils' days are long and arduous, leaving him little time for anything other than sleeping and eating, but at the moment he is on a mission to find the perfect engagement ring for Mareka. The jewellers in the local mall are out of the question, they are too pricey. Anyway the rings there are hardly unique. For Mareka it's got to be something special, something you don't see everyday.

It's nearly closing time and Emils has got a delivery to make before 5.30. The package reads *M & W Services, 55 Tollgate Square*. Finally he locates the shop. In the window are two electric guitars, a shelf of computer games and a sign saying "Gold: bought and sold" and another hastily-written sign in black marker pen which reads "Closing down today - everything must go".

The shop is virtually empty. The man behind the counter looks dreadful, as if the weight of the world was resting on his shoulders. Remembering his time target Emils throws the package onto the counter on the dot at 5.30.
'Sign here,' he says to the harassed-looking man. The man looks up, he looks like he hasn't slept for weeks. Emils wonders what might be in the package; hopefully something that will cheer this poor man up.

As he looks again at the care-worn man, something catches his eye. In a glass cabinet behind the man's head is a tray of rings. Sitting in the very middle of the centre tray is a beautiful opal ring, surrounded by diamonds. A large price tag reads £200.

'I will give you £50 for that ring' says Emils, seizing the opportunity.
'Done, it's yours!' says the man looking, for a second, strangely relieved.

7.

With the money paid, parcel delivered and ring safely stashed in his pocket, passionate Emils is impatient to declare his love. Bursting through the front door of the block of flats, that he and

Mareka live in, he sprints upstairs. Removing the flat cap, that he has recently taken to wearing, he goes down on bended knee in front of a puzzled Mareka; who is sitting on the sofa watching a game show.

Yet instead of the cooing admiration he had expected, there is a sharp intake of breath from Mareka. She is looking at the ring; which Emils is holding out in front of him.
'Don't you know that opals are unlucky?'
'But it is beautiful, please put it on…'
'No, no! I'm not wearing that!'
'But I just paid a lot of money for it!'
'Well then, you can take it back in the morning, can't you?'

A heated and passionate "discussion" ensues, the upshot of which leaves the ring deposited on the kitchen table, unwanted and unloved. In a desperate attempt to mollify the situation Emils books a table at his friend's restaurant. Hopefully he can take the ring back to the pawnbrokers in the morning….

At the restaurant the lovers' quarrel is soon forgotten; with the aid of several bottles of red wine. Songs are sung of the old country and Emils even stands on the table to once more declare his love for Mareka. With the extended opening hours, that apply uniquely to Latvian friends and family, it is past midnight before they wend their weary way home to....a smouldering heap of timbers.

In their absence that evening a fire had taken hold of their flat and soon engulfed the whole block. Fire engines had arrived at the scene, but had arrived too late to do anything other than hose down the smouldering timbers and the blackened skeletal furniture; which now sits stranded amongst the rubble. Mercifully no-one has been hurt. Clad only in their nightclothes and clutching a few of their most cherished possessions the other residents of the flats sit sorrowfully at the roadside. As for Emils and Mareka they have only the clothes they are standing up in and...each other. As for the ring, its existence has been temporarily forgotten.

8.

The Relationship Coastguards: let us steer your relationship away from the rocks. It doesn't matter whether you are newly-weds, or have been in a relationship for years; relationships sometimes founder and we are here to guide you safely on your way. We can see you separately for one-to-one sessions, or as a couple; where you can explore your relationship safely with our counsellor acting as a friendly go-between and mediator...

Sessions available with one of our select crew; please contact us for further details. relationshipcoastguards@gmail.com .

Some months have passed. With the help of a local counselling service Amanda has now returned to

Andrew, with her tail between her legs. He can see that she has been taught the lesson of her life. Ring or no ring, lover or non-existent imaginary lover, he is glad to have her home. She seems like a different person. It is almost like having a second marriage.

As for Emils, he will never disbelieve Mareka again. She told him that the ring was unlucky and now they have lost everything. The ring was left at the flat: the flat burned down. He doesn't require any greater proof of Mareka's omniscience and wisdom.

The site which housed their cramped little second floor flat has become the subject of interest for a local property developer. Their rather unsavoury landlord is happy to take the insurance money for the loss of the property. He couldn't have planned it better himself; now he's going to take his stash of cash and buy some cheaper properties elsewhere. He will start the vicious cycle of exploitation in another town; where he is not so well-known, or loathed, by the local council.

The new developers, Guinevere Homes, have sent in a wrecking crew to remove the charred timbers and the detritus left behind. Big Martin McGovern is chief wrecker and smasher-upper. A lofty chap, standing well over six foot; he could have been tailor-made for the job. He lifts up the splintered timbers with no gloves on: gloves are for wimps.

He is able to launch the timbers single-handed into the waiting skip.

Broken toilets, twisted shower fittings, the skeletons of dralon sofas, they are all treated with the same rough justice. He sends in his son, Pete, with the large yard broom to tidy the site up.
'Dad, look what I've found!'
Martin looks towards him, in Pete's hand is a small golden object.
'Look at this, it must be worth something.' Pete insists.
'You're not wrong there son. You're a chip off the old block,' says Martin, hurriedly tucking the ring away in his pocket before anyone else should see it. Martin and Pete know better than to tell their boss, Donny Adams of Guinevere Homes, about their little find.

9.

It was not long after Martin's discovery that the legendary "McGovern ring" was put up for auction at one of London's top auction houses. In an effort to disguise its provenance, Martin has gone to a great deal of trouble to cook up a back story for the ring. He has been advised that the punters love a bit of romance; so in the auction catalogue, underneath a beautiful photo of the ring, is the legend of the McGovern Opal. Allegedly it was smuggled out of Ireland in Molly McGovern's petticoats during the great potato famine. Why a penniless Irish girl would not have simply sold the ring is a question which one might think wouldn't bear too much scrutiny.

The local regional TV station has taken an interest and their roving reporter, David Mohammed, is camped outside the auction rooms. His colleague, Sally Mansfield, is questioning him from the comfort of the TV studio.

'David, where do we find you today?' she asks, smiling the broadest of smiles.

'Hello there Sally. Yes, I'm here today because of one item that has come up for sale at Waterby's auction rooms. The legendary McGovern Opal ring, which has been handed down through the McGovern family for centuries. This beautiful ring is being sought after by many buyers including, it is rumoured, Prince Frederick of Luxembourg. If his bid is successful his wife, the former Princess Maria-Luisa of San Marino, will be the lucky recipient. If you remember she is due to give birth any day now, what more fitting gift could a loving husband give than this amazing sparkler?'

At this point a picture flashed up on the screen showing a beautiful gold ring featuring a large opal surrounded by diamonds. In the front room of a reasonably desirable semi-detached home in Ladyfield, near Westgate, Andrew Ellis is watching the local news. At the sight of the ring his jaw hits the floor. He summons Amanda, who is in the next room.

'Manda, Manda, I just saw *that* ring on the TV. They're putting it up for auction'. Amanda turns a

whiter shade of pale, remembering her recent troubles, and says
'My God, it's got to be stopped, that ring is cursed'.

Back inside the TV studio Sally Mansfield is still talking about the ring.
'Now, we've had a few calls today warning that opals are bad luck and some even more outlandish claims, that I'm afraid just don't merit air time. Anyway if your cash is burning a hole in your pocket, the auction is due to take place at Waterby's at 5pm today. Tune in this evening and see who triumphs in the auction battle…'

Inside the auction rooms that afternoon the phones rang as never before. Little Izzy Mayfield, who was there on work experience after completing her degree in Fine Art, hung up the phone in exasperation and said to her colleague, Alex,
'We've had an another of those crank callers, it's the fifth one I've had today, claiming that the opal ring is bad luck' 'Bloody hell, what superstitious nonsense' said Alex, 'some people will swallow anything'.

Later on that afternoon David Mohammed is once again bright-eyed and bushy-tailed outside the auction rooms. As he turns once again to the camera he breaks the news,
'And I'm standing here outside Waterby's where we've just heard that the English National Museum have put in a record bid for the ring. They now believe it to be *the* ring that is at the centre of an

infamous Wessex legend, involving a woman who was burned as a witch. Known as the "Ring of Unluck" it will be securely housed in a bomb-proof cabinet with triple-strength, glass. That should satisfy those amongst you who are believers in such things as superstitions and folk tales.'

Martin McGovern, former employee of Guinevere Homes and weaver of tall tales, has no shame. After all he was told to give the ring a bit of a back story. As long as he receives the money for the sale, he's happy to twist that tale a bit further so that it also contains a witch. He'll be on his way to the Maldives next week with the proceeds; it's no expense spared for the McGovern family from now on.

10.

The ring was both stunning and beautiful and for several months it brought in record revenues for the museum. The once-abandoned village of Godmanshurst and its Saxon church went from strength to strength. The removal of the ring by the unwitting Amanda seemed to have led to almost overnight financial prosperity for the surrounding area. Previously abandoned hamlets nearby are suddenly highly sought after and property prices have spiked. Even the fields around the church, which have been barren for centuries, have suddenly brought forth bumper crops of wheat and barley. Godmanshurst's association with the "Ring of Unluck" only seems to bring in more publicity and that is never a bad thing. There are several British TV crews in the area today and lots of interest from abroad. Just as Graham Mallory's wife predicted, he will soon be fronting a TV special on the History channel.

However, he is still eager to see the artefact for himself. His professional pride has been wounded; especially when he remembers how quickly that silly woman in the flowery wellingtons left the dig. As he looks at the beautiful jewelled ring, safely housed behind the triple-strength security glass, he feels an unholy pull of envy and a sickness rising in his gullet. If only he had found it first....

As he turns to go home, he still feels under the ring's magical and malign influence. He imagines the glory that could have been his; if only he had discovered it first. He sighs audibly, as he stumbles in a daze down the stone steps outside the museum.

It's closing time now, each display cabinet is checked and the display rooms are locked and sealed off to the public. Finally the museum director closes the huge double doors and hands over to the night time security staff in their booth outside.

As the clock strikes twelve, that traditional witching hour, the peace and quiet of the museum is torn apart by the ear-piercing sound of a woman's scream. A scream which has travelled across the centuries to be here. Upstairs in room 432 the triple-strength security glass of the bomb-proof cabinet starts to shatter into silvery splinters. The Ring of Unluck starts to quake and vibrate. Once again it is surrounded by the familiar smell of burning, for the third time in just over five hundred years.

Lunex Insurance Services
by
Lizzie Jarrett

1.

The towns of Westgate and Hursterham were only eight miles apart, but they were as different from one another as you could imagine.

Whilst the people of Hursterham liked to imagine that they were socially and intellectually superior to the people in the new town of Westgate; this aspiration was somewhat undermined by the arrival, once a day at the local bus station, of a motley crew of residents from the surrounding villages.

From Nether's End came a very large tribe; a mother, a father and seven of their children. All with the same shade of red hair, the same squashed nose and the same large cold blue eyes. Then, from Laughton only five miles further on, all the residents, it would seem, were over six foot tall. Their hair grew in a tangle-top of brown curls, from under which one could see the same mud-green eyes and prominent beak-like noses. Not to be outdone were the people from the village of Ploughley with their cross-eyed, boss-eyed children each with identical dull grey skin and mousey-straight hair. And, let us not forget, even within Hursterham itself, many residents seem to be possessed of that distinctive physical gift that is the "Hursterham Chin".

A local tourist guide book, written by a proud Hursterham resident has this to say about his home town.

Hursterham is a prosperous town in the county of Sussex that can date its origins back to Saxon times. Many of the town's residents have ancestry that has remained within Hursterham over many centuries. There are many ancient buildings in Hursterham, but despite this, the town was totally omitted from the Domesday book. Obviously this omission was a gross oversight by the King's emissaries…

Excerpt from Hursterham, the Jewel of Sussex by Ray Richardson, available at selected booksellers.

The number of people from the nearby new town of Westgate that could trace their ancestry back within the town, or even to Sussex itself, are few and far between. Instead they were the children, or grandchildren, of dockers and match girls from the East End or newer arrivals from the Indian subcontinent, or even more far flung provinces.

The people of Westgate could be said to be classless, since they had arrived in this audacious little town with nothing but their wits to help them on their way. Many of them had now prospered with the benefit of well-planned housing, clean water and the safe streets of this 1960s new town. Their children had enjoyed the benefits of a comprehensive education, regular dental checks, conveniently located GP services and a brand new hospital, they even had a purpose built shopping centre to spend their pocket money in. The young people of Westgate had never had it so good; it's just that they weren't all aware of the benefits they were enjoying.

The people of Hursterham had continued on in a slight time warp, one class not mixing with the other and the children of the town being sent to single sex schools, which were either grammar or secondary modern. There was a place for everyone and everyone should know their place. This sorry and sad status quo was maintained by the powers that be and the town stagnated.

Incidentally, the real reason for Hursterham being omitted from the Domesday book was, and still would be, due to the excellence of the local breweries. Such was the potency of the local beer, that the King's representatives had drunk themselves into a stupor. Upon waking the next day they had omitted the town from the record due to shame and a complete lack of memory of the town and its existence.

Parts of ancient Westgate were actually recorded in the Domesday book; since there had been a settlement there since the bronze age. However, it was not until the building of the new town that Westgate started to spread its wings and threatened to challenge the status of its more historic neighbour.

It was in Hursterham however, and not Westgate, that the insurance company Lunex chose to have its head offices and, as is so often the case with Hursterham, many family members chose to work at Lunex so they need never be far from one another.

2.

Dear Customer

At Lunex Insurance Services we offer you security and reassurance. By taking out a policy with Lunex you are assured of protection from financial misery should the worst happen. We offer many different categories of insurance including Life Assurance, Mortgage protection, Home Insurance and Motor Insurance.

Should the type of insurance you are searching for not have been mentioned above; please do not hesitate to contact us and we will endeavour to answer your query.

Yours faithfully

Simon de Jong
Managing Director
Lunex Insurance Services

In section H on the second floor of the browny-grey, pebble-dash effect tower block that housed Lunex Insurance Services, Maidy McDonald sat at the top of her table lovingly watching over her team. Her over-sized lenses, encased in their tortoiseshell effect plastic frames, gave her the appearance of a rather elderly mother owl. She lovingly watched their every move and attempted to extend to them, when she could, the benefit of her many years of experience in the insurance industry. On occasion she would impart some sage and sanguine words of advice about life and how to deal with its many challenges.

Having come to Hursterham from Dundee with her husband, Dougie, Maidy had now been a widow for over thirty years. But with typical courage and vigour she had soldiered on and brought up her sons, Dougie junior and Davey, on her own. Dougie now lived in London, where he worked as a hospital consultant. However, with Dougie never able to return her telephone calls and Davey (well, who knew where he was), Maidy had transferred her maternal feelings to her work. She regarded every member of Section H as a member of her extended family.

She had risen to a reasonable rank of seniority within the company. Within Section H she was second in command, answerable only to Mr. Johnson; who had his own office with a window that looked out over the local park.

Unfortunately at this moment Mr. Johnson had his back to the window, but if he had turned round, in his comfortable swivel chair, he would have seen two new recruits approaching the building.

Walking from his very nicely appointed home, on a very pleasant and leafy avenue barely five minutes away, is Michael. He preferred to be known by any new acquaintances as Mik. He is very smartly attired, wearing a teal blue tie over a stylish slate grey shirt. He sports fashionably tight blue trousers over his jet black leather winkle-picker shoes. His flirtatious baby blue eyes contrast with a very stylish and scrupulously maintained quiff. He is soon to be on first name terms with all of the ladies in the office.

From a completely different direction and rushing along the main road from the station comes Joanna. She's just got off the train from Westgate and she's determined not to be late on her first day at work. She is wearing what she thinks *people wear in offices;* wobbling along in high heels and wearing the only smart blouse and skirt she owns. She feels desperately uncomfortable and looks and feels a good twenty years older than her eighteen years.

For both of them it is their first day *ever* at work.

Joanna had recently left school having gained some very average A levels. She was planning to earn some money before taking up a place at teacher training college the following September. But not yet being in possession of a required pass grade in

Maths, she might very well be grateful, in twelve months time, of a steady and well-paid job in a local insurance company.

Mik, on the other hand, had equally atrocious A levels, however he had no intention of doing anything worthy or sensible. But he did need to be out of the family home during the day and taking a temporary job with this established insurance company seemed like a good idea…to his parents. What was going on in Mik's mind was another thing entirely. This was what Lunex Insurance Solutions were going to find out…eventually.

Neither Joanna or Mik had any pretensions whatsoever to work long-term in the insurance industry, but there are different ways of conveying that message: that which doesn't convey any offence and that which does.

3.

On their first day at the company Joanna and Mik spent the day getting to know their colleagues. They were both shown how to sign in, where to get lunch and what time they were expected to turn up for work and when they could leave. They were introduced to their instructors, Stephanie and Enid, and shown a few basics of the job. It seemed to be a matter of filling in random and unrelated letters and numbers onto various unrelated paper forms; which were themselves known by an equally confusing combination of letters and numbers that made sense to someone... but definitely not to them.

Joanna's new mentor, Stephanie Stevens, had been with Lunex since the day she left school. Her life revolved around her ailing body. Every day another fresh ailment; one day cystitis, the next day a cold that wouldn't dry up. The following week she had a "funny tummy" and the next week she had a bad back. Some of these ailments were genuine and some were not. The truth was that, deep down inside, she had never intended to return to work after having children; it was just that she couldn't acknowledge that to herself, or to her husband.

Enid Riddles, Mik's instructor, had been with Lunex for as long as Maidy had. But whereas Maidy had made use of her time there to educate herself and forge good working relationships, Enid had used her time at Lunex to thoroughly exhaust the goodwill of anyone with whom she came into contact.

Was Enid a woman possessed of any sense whatsoever?
No.
Was she someone to whom a young man of eighteen could look up to?
No.
Was this the only way Maidy could find to keep Enid gainfully occupied and out of her way for several weeks?
Yes.

On the second day Joanna caught the train in from nearby Westgate, clocked in on time and was seated by the time Mik squeaked in at one minute past nine.

Joanna did not enjoy her days at work, they were deadly dull and Stephanie's explanation of the purpose of the form filling did nothing to make the job any more interesting or compelling. Mik, on the other hand, was having a whale of a time surrounded by predominantly middle-aged ladies. They were simply delighted to have a young man in their midst; whether they would continue to think this for much longer was anyone's guess.

By the end of the first week Joanna's opinion of Lunex was now beginning to harden. It was not a place where she would be making her future career, the only thing that livened it up was the new boy. By day five Mik's attempts to arrive on time had been totally abandoned. He was there by 9.15 or 9.20 most days. His smart black overcoat, for which a hanger was provided, lay stranded on the floor of the staff wardrobe, in a sartorial attempt to undermine the authority of the hanger.

Something unexpected happened on the Friday morning: a letter turned up. Not a nice little letter informing ex-colleagues about someone's progress in their new career, nor indeed a boring little letter asking for bank account details or a forwarding address, but a very nasty little letter indeed.

Mr. A. Johnson
Section H, 2nd Floor
Lunex Insurance Services
Britannia Road
Hursterham

Mr. Johnson,

What a fat, pompous fool you are. Your wife can't stand you and would leave you if she could. She spends most of her days ogling the sixth-formers at the Sir Edward Ferroner College. I wonder what else she gets up to? No wonder she looks so tired! Makes you think, doesn't it?

Expect more communications soon.

A friend

P.S. The suit you wear to work is awful.

Mr. Johnson was the senior controller of section H and he was a creature of habit. He turned up every day at the same time and went into his office on the other side of the corridor. He wore the same brown suit and he smelt of tobacco and a distinctly middle of the range after-shave. On Friday nights he would go for a pint or two with some of the other section controllers. Saturdays meant shopping with his wife in town and then football on the television in the afternoon. On Sundays he would sleep late and then his wife would cook a very large roast dinner for Mr. Johnson and their son, Andrew. Mrs. Johnson would sigh and idly pick at a salad, whilst her boys tucked into their dinners. Mrs. Johnson longed for a more exciting life, whereas Mr. Johnson did not like surprises. But Mr. Johnson was not aware of the way others saw him, or the fact that his wife might not be satisfied with her life; he was very, very surprised and felt rather sad.

He wondered who could have sent such a letter. It was very specific; he felt as if he were being watched. However, as head of section, he decided that no-one else need to know about the contents of the letter; after all maybe they wouldn't write again? Looking carefully around him, to see he wasn't being observed, he pushed the letter to the very bottom of the drawer and deposited a lot of Lunex Insurance Services pre-paid envelopes on top of it.

4.

The following Monday a very strange green-haired figure rolled in late to the office. It was Mik. He now sported a mohican hair cut. This radical style of haircut is hard enough to carry off even for the most chiselled jaw, drop-dead gorgeous specimen of manhood, but the fact that he had also dyed his hair a very unattractive shade of green, simply made the attention-seeking teenager look sickly and ill.

From then on his card was marked. Maidy, a grandmotherly figure, had at least a sense of humour about the whole thing. She could see that Mik's behaviour was designed to provoke and offend and she was not going to play along.

Enid, on the other had, was in a state of high dudgeon. She felt that his refusal to conform to her expectations of how a young man should behave undermined the very foundations of Western society. She took it very personally.
'Well, who does he think he is, wearing his hair like that? Why can't he hang his coat up? It upsets me so'.

Enid had been married at nineteen to a man who was by blinded by her "lively" personality and perhaps by her svelte figure. He had found out the hard way that some other words that also applied to Enid were "irritating" and "feeble-minded".

She still had a slim figure though. She regularly boasted, to all that would listen, about her adherence to foundation garments which gave her a very wasp-waisted look. However, the glamorous look she aspired to was marred by the vacant expression that loomed out from behind the square black frames of her glasses. With her long spindly legs and her formless mouth, which often hung open, she resembled a slightly gormless frog rather than the fashion plate she hoped to be.

After several years of marriage and no children (at Enid's insistence), her husband had finally left her for another woman. The effect of this desertion on

Enid was profound, it was pretty much her sole topic of conversation; other than extolling the virtues of foundation wear.

By virtue of her years of service in the company Enid should really have been third in command under Maidy. However, this position had been taken instead by Avis Devers. Enid could simply not have been trusted. Avis was a stylish woman of about fifty-five with a carefully maintained bob, which she paid vast quantities of money to a local hairdresser to maintain. Nobody ever asked what had happened to Mr. Devers; they were too afraid to ask.

Avis was very happy working at Lunex, since she could see her son, Stevie, on a daily basis. He was a computer programmer there. She also liked to "drop in" on her son in the evenings, so she could keep an eye on her grandchildren.

Stevie's wife, Gaynor, was not so happy with this arrangement and was not enjoying life as Avis's daughter-in-law. She also worked at Lunex, which is where she had met her husband, but now she worked in section H, alongside her very strong-minded mother-in-law.

Apart from Mik, the men in the office kept a pretty low profile. Mr. Johnson, the section head, was usually very happy with his lot, when he wasn't receiving unpleasant letters, that is. There was a pleasant red-haired chap called Danny, who played the saxophone in his spare time and definitely planned to leave at some time in the not too distant future. Lunex did not feature too much in his long-term plans. Sitting opposite Danny was Jamie. In his mid-thirties, he was still on the look-out for a wife. His big brown eyes and lovely manners were a big plus in his favour, however, on the down-side, his devotion to his elderly parents meant that he still lived at home. Jamie hoped that he would still find that special someone within the confines of Lunex Insurance Services.

However, on the Friday morning another letter arrived: nobody in section H could rest easy it would seem.

5.

Lunex Insurance Services
Second Floor, Section H

Snivelling Stephanie,

Your husband should leave you. I know you weren't ill the other day, you were in Bellman's department store having a cup of tea and a scone.

Avis, your daughter-in-law doesn't like you as much you think she does. She and your son are planning to move to Westgate and send their children to a comprehensive school.

Don't forget there will be another letter soon.

From your concerned friend.

The following Monday arrived and the majority of the office had made up their minds that the nasty letter must have come from one of the newcomers and Mik was the obvious suspect. Enid had spent several evenings coming up with, what she thought were, some stinging phrases that would cut him down to size. She needn't have wasted her time, because on Monday Mik did not turn up to work. Tuesday came and still no green-haired teenager. On Wednesday Mr. Johnson was able to announce that Mik would not be continuing with section H and that everyone should return to their work as normal. However, nobody got any work done that day because they all wanted to have their two penny worth; about what they would have said to the young wastrel had he been there.

Many of them had not liked Mik, he had been everything they were not. He had been vibrant, lively and fun, they were none of these things. Maidy had always had a feeling that this was how things would end. She had enjoyed his presence in the office, she also understood that he must have been a very unhappy young man to have sought so much attention.

Speculation was rife; how was Mik getting all this information? It certainly was accurate; you could tell that from the stunned looks on Stephanie and

Avis's faces. Mik's girlfriend, Camilla, worked on the ground floor as a receptionist. Perhaps she was passing him the information?

It was with a sigh of relief that section H came into work on Thursday morning. Now with Mik, the giant cuckoo, removed from the nest everyone could just settle back into their nice little cosy routine. Indeed by Friday morning, when he still had not returned, there was a feeling of elation, bordering on intoxication in the department. Let normality reign again.

6.

Over in Westgate the local teenagers were looking forward to Saturday night. Released from the shackles of school for the weekend they were ready to cut loose. There was a triple bill of local bands playing tonight at one of the local community centres. Top of the bill would be The Lord of the Fleas, all the way from Hursterham. Providing support would be Peace Riot and also, from Joanna's old school, The Agents of Death.

Joanna was resplendent in her Saturday night outfit, her curly hair fiercely backcombed into a huge mane. Her very highest high heels were matched with some extremely tight jeans and a purple mohair jumper. Her friends, Tina and Sharon, were likewise dressed to kill. This was the night when the bored youth of Westgate got together and tested their tolerance of beer, cider, vodka and whatever else they could get their hands on. The bands on the stage tested the strength of their amplifiers and the tolerance of those poor locals who lived nearest to the community centre.

By the time the girls arrived at the community centre, Peace Riot were on their last number. From the dribble of applause at the end it sounded as if they hadn't missed much. The Agents of Death featured a boy the girls had gone to school with as their lead singer. Their music was pretty much as their name suggested and after one song the girls had retreated outside for a smoke in the pub garden. Then suddenly at 10.30 there was a sudden rush to the stage as Lord of the Fleas made their entrance. To the chorus of "O Fortuna" from "Carmina Burana", a familiar face stood facing Joanna; as the stage lighting shone red onto the heavily made-up face of Mik. His band gave an outstanding performance, which concluded with him kissing a pig's head; brought to him on a platter by his girlfriend, who was dressed as a very sexy waitress.

Making her excuses to Tina and Sharon, Joanna stayed behind until the stage was clear, so she could talk to the Lord of the Fleas himself. She had nearly given up when the band emerged from behind the stage, heading for the car park.
'Beats scaring old ladies, doesn't it?' she said.
'What do you mean?' said the strangely-civilised face of Mik, now that his face was clear of stage make-up.

'The letters, that was you, wasn't it?...I mean who else would do it?'
Mik took a deep breath and looked her straight in the eye and said
'What do you mean "who else"? That place is full of weirdos, take your pick!'
Joanna thought for a moment, she was right, he had a point.

7.

So it was no surprise to Joanna when on Monday morning another letter arrived; it certainly seemed to surprise everyone else.
'But I don't understand...' said Avis to Enid 'that boy isn't here anymore, this shouldn't be happening...'.
Yet still the letter sat there with no-one brave enough to open it.
'You open it Joanna, it won't be about you,' said Avis.

She was right, it wasn't about her, it was about Maidy. Joanna handed the letter over. The correct recipient perused the letter, sighed and looked sadly over her over-sized glasses.
'It's someone's sad idea of a blackmail letter,' said Maidy in her lovely Scottish burr.
'Call the Police' said Mr. Johnson, 'I've had quite enough of this.'

Of course, in a sense, it was too late, the magical glue that had kept section H together for so many years was now starting to dissolve. Mr. Johnson had received several requests from people asking to be moved to different departments within Lunex and the revelations about Avis's son and daughter-in-law had only forced their hand. The family were moving away and now Avis was just a miserable elderly single lady, who would no longer have access to her grandchildren. Her unhappiness was palpable.

8.

It is a beautiful sun-drenched day in June and in the back garden of 119 Lambs Down Lane the residents are setting up for a barbecue. The birds are singing, the flowers are dancing in the breeze and the green grass ripples like great green waves on a great green sea. In the garden next door however, no birds are singing and there are no flowers. If the sun could penetrate through the prison walls of laurel and leylandii it would immediately be swallowed up by the concrete desert that serves as the back garden.

Inside a lonely woman sits at the breakfast table. The house is just as her husband left it fifteen years ago. She has not removed his place setting from the breakfast table, some of his clothes still hang in the wardrobe upstairs. Two of his suits still get sent to the dry cleaners once a year, just in case. On the table in front of the woman sits a pile of notepaper. At the head of the page there is a

picture of a winsome puppy. In the background the telephone answering service switches on.
'Hallo, this is Howard and Enid. We're not home at the moment, but if you want to leave a message, we'll get back to you'.

Enid has become emboldened; in her tiny and fragile mind everybody at work is against her, but they need to be taught a lesson. She knows things, she overhears things, she sees things. People need to know what is going on behind their backs. They need Enid, she must help them. After her previous friendly words of advice have been ignored, she has decided that a little gentle blackmail may help them see the light.

While she waits to see what effect her note to Maidy will have, Enid decides to go for an easy target. Poor lonely Avis has been enjoying a dalliance with an unknown man at a local car boot sale. Avis needs to be warned about this kind of behaviour, maybe she might listen this time…after all she wouldn't want everyone else in the department to know. Five pounds a week should ensure total silence; after all moral indiscretions should be punished. She picks up a piece of winsome puppy paper and clamps it into the roller of the typewriter.

In the background the phone starts to ring, it goes through to the answerphone after two rings.
'Hallo, this is Howard and Enid. We're not home at the moment….' the message continued.

The beep sounded and then a voice that Enid knew well came on the line.

'Enid, Enid, this is Howard. I've asked you repeatedly, please remove my name from your answerphone message. Also, stop writing to Caroline. I left you fifteen years ago. It is my fault and my fault alone….'

A woman's voice could be heard in the background.

'Howard, Howard, are you on the phone to that woman again? Put the phone down!'

'Yes, dear,' said the man, there was a dull click as the handset at the other end was replaced.

Enid smiled contentedly. She loved the way Howard continued to stay in touch. Deep down inside he must still care for her.

Now, with another blackmail letter primed and ready to go, she's off on her rounds. That friendly note she sent to Maidy should have had its desired effect by now. She'll be off to pick up her payment; as soon as the shops close and there are less people on the streets.

A short walk away on the edge of the town centre is a public convenience. It is to be the stage and setting for the handover of the blackmail money. A nice little payment for Enid to keep secret about a family scandal or a dirty secret. On the door of the third cubicle along a note on the door reads "Out of order". All Enid has to do is push open the door and she will find a plain brown envelope secreted behind the toilet cistern containing the money.

9.

Maidy McDonald had been very puzzled when she first opened the letter addressed to her, why would anyone think that she was ashamed of any of her grandchildren? Her second son, Davey, was very generous in his affections, so it was no surprise to Maidy to find that she was to be a grandmother once again.

Apparently the latest recipient of Davey's libidinous loins was that nice little Sikh girl from the greengrocers. Certainly Meena Kaur's parents were not that pleased, but in time they would accept this extra-pale little grandchild.

However, at this very moment in time, the thought that perplexes Maidy was why anyone thought she would pay money to keep little Govinder's parentage a secret.

Police Sergeant Emma Conley and Constable Jack Price have advised her to play along with the blackmailer. With this in mind, Maidy has placed an empty plain brown envelope in the third cubicle of the public conveniences in King's Street. The Sergeant and the Constable are going to keep an eye on things and see who turns up.

10.

Enid pushes open the door of the third cubicle. The notice reading "Out of order" looks really professional and extremely convincing. But inside there is just an obviously faulty toilet, with the lid down and a bin placed on top of it. No brown envelope anywhere to be seen. In her frustration she checks all the other cubicles.

As she searches frantically she hears a creaking noise, the door outside is being closed. Before she can get to the door she hears a key being turned in the lock. The council employee has jumped into their van and driven off. The Queen's Street conveniences are always locked early, those in King's Street won't be locked until much later. In her greed and confusion Enid had forgotten that she had typed "King's Street" on her note to Maidy, not "Queen's Street", but now it is far too late.

Sergeant Conley and PC Price are disappointed to find that their sting operation has backfired. Obviously there is nothing inside the plain brown envelope which has been placed inside the third cubicle along. But nobody has turned up to claim the envelope either, they have been double-crossed.

11.

It's Saturday night and Mik and his friends are making their way home from a successful gig. They've stopped at the pub for a pint or three and are now in a very good mood, although not quite sober. They've just cut across the street and have left Mik on his own at the bottom of Queen's

Street, he's had more than enough to drink and there's quite a racket going on in his head, but even so he thinks he can hear a woman's voice. It is a familiar voice, a wheedling, irritating tone, one that he had come to detest.

'Let me out, let me out!' says the strange disembodied voice.

Whilst their sting operation has so far been unsuccessful, Sergeant Conley and PC Price are still determined to catch their blackmailer. They have phoned all Lunex employees this evening in an effort to work out who the culprit might be, but they were unable to get an answer from Enid's phone. A visit to her house is in order. From the outside it looks unremarkable, a knock at the door results in no response. After ten minutes trying to get an answer, big Jack Price applies the *shoulder technique* and then the *boot technique* to force the door open.

The hallway is immaculate and the carpet is hoovered to perfection. Opening the door through to the kitchen and lounge area reveals a different story. A tiny, upright typewriter sits on the kitchen table. There is a piece of paper already behind the roller, a sad and winsome puppy looks up from the page. The top line is addressed to Avis, Section H, Second Floor, Lunex Insurance Services.

Pinned up around both rooms are clippings from local newspapers, mostly bad news stories; obituaries and court reports. The answerphone in

the lounge area is flashing. Emma pushes the "play" button, a message plays.
'For God's sake Enid leave Caroline alone, she's never done anything to hurt you.' From the looks of things the employees of Lunex are not the only people this woman doesn't like. A card index system on the dresser is most informative. It details Enid's victims, their "crimes" and the date that Enid has contacted them. Finally on the bottom line it notes *"paid £..."* or *"unpaid, to be recontacted"*. But Enid herself is nowhere to be seen.

Outside the Queen's Street public conveniences a strange young man, rather tipsy and still wearing the trademark red stage make-up from the gig, is balancing on the edge of a low wall. In doing this he is able to peer down into the window of the Queen's Street toilets. Cowering on the floor is the familiar spindly legged, wasp-waisted figure of a very odd middle-aged lady.
'Whoever you are. Please take pity on me and let me out…' she appeals.
In the dark of the night she is unable to see the strange red-stained face of her teenage nemesis looking in at her.

Mik is enjoying this sudden turn in his fortunes. He has complete power over Enid. What should he do? Should he be sensible and just open the door or should he have some fun first? He doesn't know whether he should listen to his conscience or discard its advice and have some fun.

'Enid. Enid, I know it's you. If I let you out, do you promise never to judge people because of their appearance again?'

'Yes, I promise'

'Enid, do you promise never to talk about your ex-husband or your foundation wear again?'

'Yes, I promise, but hurry up the police will be here soon...'

Sensing the unique opportunity to right a wrong, Mik decides to mete out a bit of natural justice.

'Enid, when the door is opened. I want you to promise to walk straight to the train station and get on the first train you find. Don't ever come back, we don't want weirdos like you in Hursterham!'

12.

Sergeant Emma Conley and PC Jack Price concluded their case within the week. There were no more strange letters to Section H of Lunex Insurance Services. After several years Enid's house, 121 Lamb's Down Road, was sold and Howard and Caroline received a nice little sum. Mik settled down and eventually married his girlfriend, Camilla; she's doing really well at Lunex and should soon become a Section Manager. It's funny how quickly she achieved promotion.

Mik can pretty much do as he likes. Having fulfilled his side of the parental bargain to see what it was like working at the family firm; he can fill his days pursuing his pop career. Mik De Jong, known only to his family as Michael, just has to present himself at the Lunex Insurance Services board meetings once every six months, being a non-executive board member is really hard work...

A limited search was made for Enid, but it was concluded at an early stage. With no dependants there was no-one to nag or chastise the police and they do have very limited resources. Perhaps Lunex Insurance Services and the citizens of Hursterham are better off without her...

Westgate Weekly News

Strange messages found in library books.

Police are baffled by strange messages being found in library books issued from Westgate library. The content varies, but they are usually highly-moralising in tone and often threaten or attempt to blackmail their target. It is unknown how the perpetrator manages to find out which book will be chosen, but the personal information known by the perpetrator about his victim is thought to be uncannily accurate.

If you think you know who the perpetrator might be, please ring the following number in confidence....

The Way Forward?
by
Lizzie Jarrett

1.

Welcome to Westgate College.

Westgate College is proud to be a leader in the Creative Arts. Whilst we are extremely proud of our Maths, English and Science Departments, special care is taken at Westgate to involve all children in the Creative Arts; all students must take at least one Arts based GCSE. At Westgate we value individuality, you will never be treated like educational clones.

As the latest supply teacher entered the room an empty can whistled through the air and hit her square in the face. The woman winced. She didn't have to be doing this, she thought to herself, but at the same time she knew this to be a lie. There were bills to be paid, children to be fed and clothed and a single mother cannot be choosy.

Upstairs in the headteacher's office, a meeting was taking place. On the desk was a large brown envelope marked "CONFIDENTIAL", inside were the rather damning results of the latest Ofteach inspection. On the wall was a photo showing the current headmaster shaking hands with a previous prime minister, both men were smiling broadly. Today, the headmaster's face betrayed a completely different set of emotions.
'We're dangerously close to being put into special measures and then...you know what that means....', said Mr. Ryan to his second-in-command, Ms. Simmonds, an intelligent young

woman in her early thirties. The head looked inquisitively at his deputy, was this woman after his job? Did she really think she could do the job instead? Well, for two pins she could have the job!

But Ms. Simmonds did *not* want the job, she was quite comfortable doing what she was doing, thank you very much and she thought she did it well. She was happy in her life and she loved the subject she taught. She loved the school and she loved the children she worked with.

2.

Welcome to the XLSys Academy Trust where we embrace the future. XLSys has a bold new vision of a multi-academy organisation working in harmony with industry and embracing new technology. Aiming for academic excellence at all time, we accept no compromise either from our staff or from our students. With calculated investment in all technology based subjects, we aim to reach for the stars with our bold and ambitious learning framework. XLSys Academy Trust: where "excellence" is the only acceptable word.

At the edge of a large industrial estate in the neighbouring town of Hawking, a tall, balding man sat in his office, poring over a map of schools in the Sussex and Surrey area. Keith Murray, director of the XLSys Academy Trust, had plans for Westgate College. The trust had already taken over St. Ursula's High School for Girls in Hawking, now Mr. Murray had Westgate College in his sights.

His first step was to get his daughter-in-law, Alison Murray, onto the board of governors at the Community College. She wasted no time and within the passing of a couple of weeks Mr. Ryan was being undermined from within.

Dear Fellow Governors

Thank you for the friendly welcome you have all extended to me. As a mother I am a firm believer in strong leadership. My husband, Samuel, and I have tried to be strong leaders to our children. I would expect a similar role model to exist in their school life. Am I wrong or is that strong leadership not being shown in our own dear school? I would like to propose that this school consider conversion to academy status. I would be delighted to recommend XLSys Academy Trust and would be happy to invite Mr. Keith Murray, director of XLSys, to attend our very next meeting.

With very best wishes

Alison

Of course there were some people whose opinion didn't count: the students. In some ways they could hold themselves partially responsible for the change in the school's fortunes, after all somebody had thrown a can at a supply teacher and somebody else had definitely reduced the head of art to a blubbering wreck.

Of course the majority of students were well-behaved young people who just wanted to come to school to see their friends. However, because of the behaviour of a small minority the school was shortly to lose Mr. Ryan, the current head. Mr. Ryan, who, for all his faults, was a pleasant enough man who had made the mistake of entering teaching because he actually liked young people. The Deputy Head, Ms. Simmonds, would follow shortly behind; she was not going to hang about here if the school was going to be academised.

3.

Speculation was rife amongst the staff as to who would be taking over. Rumours were rife, the staff and governors put forward their various preferred candidates, but finally, and without enough real scrutiny, the XLSys Academy Trust took over. Keith Murray decided that this school should get extra special treatment and that he would be the headteacher from now on.

The first day of the new term arrived and the staffroom was teeming with excitement as the teachers nervously filed in. There in front of them was their new boss, scowling and grey-faced.
'Blimey, he looks a barrel of laughs!' said John Harrison, a usually laid-back Geography teacher, but even he felt a slight twist in the pit of his

stomach as he said these words. His friend, Gregory Hughes, the Physics teacher, looked back at him: early retirement seemed ever more enticing.

Over at St.Ursula's the children had started to notice that new staff joining the school were…well, quite strange indeed. At the end of the large term, shortly after XLSys had taken over, many of the old staff had left the school. Some had taken early retirement, whilst others had made a career change and a few had even decided they would try their hand at primary education. This had left a large void to fill, a significant number of posts were being abolished altogether, but there were still a few teachers who were annoyingly irreplaceable. The school tried by bringing in lots of teacher training graduates and also staff from overseas, but inevitably there were some gaps they could not fill, so they had to bring in agency staff. It was these staff that were the strangest of all, because they were *not* human.

Supply Line, the education agency, has the latest solution in classroom management. Our range of teachers and classroom assistants are the latest in robot technology.
The MK2000 English teacher model, specialises in stock phrases and has up-to-date classroom knowledge of current teaching acronyms.
The MK5000 Maths teacher, is an authoritarian and will tolerate no talking in classrooms. Expect immediate results, in terms of productivity.

The MK1000 Music teacher, this is soon to be replaced and is expected to be largely redundant in the future. 25% price discount available for a limited time.
The Helper 9000, this is in our budget range of classroom management. Can be used either as a Teaching Assistant or Cover Supervisor. It is possible to staff the whole school with this model, it could be an extremely cost-efficient way of running a school.

4.

Back at Westgate College the first staff meeting of the new academic year was still in progress. Mr. Murray, noted Mr. Hughes and Mr. Harrison, was an expert in the use of stock phrases and clichés. Mr. Hughes had counted up five incidences of the word "tranche" whilst Mr. Harrison had "drilled down" on the use of the phrase "drill down" and had noted at least six uses of the word already.

Today many new teachers were being introduced to their colleagues. Mr. Harrison thought that many of them looked as if they had been formed from a giant jelly mould that was labelled "grey, boring, lifeless and compliant".

The MK2000, Mr. Wallis, was a rather featureless middle-aged man who had been brought in to be the new head of English, it was difficult to imagine how he could possibly have the gravitas to control even Year 7s, let alone stroppy Year 11s. It was hard to imagine that he was going to be head of department. The MK5000, Ms. Warshawski, was a stony-faced woman, possibly mid-fifties, whose forehead was deeply furrowed. It was hard to imagine that she had ever smiled.

There were three new teaching assistants, all in their mid-twenties; apparently they had *amazing* classroom management skills and could step in to cover for staff at five minutes notice, should they need to. They all had degrees and one of them even had a Masters in "The Magical World of Harry Potter".

Memos had started to appear on the noticeboard with alarming regularity; they were covered in *education-speak* to the point that no-one else outside of education would have known what the memos were about.

To all middle management - we will be meeting at 4pm every Wednesday in the staff room to drill down on your teaching techniques.
We are aiming for Sky High Inspirational Teaching and will be concentrating on being Target Oriented In Lessons and Extra Time.

One memo though was remarkably frank and the reader could have no problem understanding its central theme:
"Are you over 50? Time to be looking elsewhere?"
Mrs. Hillstrand, one of the teaching assistants, said 'Bloody cheek! Surely a woman in her fifties is in her prime?'

However, this memo was actually aimed at the teachers. The meetings were to take place straight after school in the headteacher's office. It had not been essential, so far, to get rid of teaching assistants; that initiative was to take place later on.

Mr. Hughes has been told to attend a meeting that evening. As he entered the room and saw the colour-coded folders laid out on the desk he sighed inwardly; he knew he had been failing to use this system, so strongly prescribed by Senior Leadership.

After a full hour's patronising edu-speak by the headteacher, Mr. Hughes does not need much of a push to be inwardly wording his letter of resignation. The following evening, it was the turn of Ms. Smith, fifty-eight years old and the backbone of the Languages dept. Her meeting opens with the tell-tale phrase 'Mr. Anderson was telling me how keen you are on gardening, what a shame you don't get to spend more time on your hobby.'

5.

Welcome to Watling Primary Academy, the flagship primary school for the XLSys Academy Trust. Our friendly team are eager to turn your children into life-long learners. We welcome visitors to our school and we can guarantee that they will be enthused by the energy and enthusiasm of our interstellar staff….

Clinging to the rain-swept side of a hill in the nearby town of Watling was the most miserable little primary school in either Surrey or Sussex, this is XLSys Academy's flagship primary school. The school is surrounded on both sides by the pebble-dashed horror that is Watling housing estate; flung up in a panic after the Second World War to provide homes for heroes.

One cannot help but be struck by the schism between what XLSys seeks to achieve and the fabric of the buildings in which it is operating. The poor building materials that the school is built from seemed to reinforce a feeling of misery and compromise within the school. It is one thing to aspire towards a bold new future, but all the jazzy websites and mission statements in the world cannot offset the dull reality that is Watling Primary Academy.

In Year Three the class teacher, Mrs. Datta, is scowling at her charges. She has been working late every night this week and has no energy left for her own child, Sara, who is in Year Two. Devoid of make-up and lacking in any sense of individuality or personality, her soul felt empty. Sucking down the tension even further, she launched herself upon the subject of Fronted Adverbials. The headteacher, Mrs. Heath, was very pleased with Mrs. Datta; her classes were joyless, yet thoroughly efficient.

Friendly and approachable, passionate and caring? If those four words sum you up, then there is space for you in our amazing team of support staff. What are you waiting for? Contact us today and you could soon be part of our winning team.

In the hall, an angry-eyed harridan was conducting a Phonics lesson. She barked her suppressed rage at her nine year old charges.
'Read the word, repeat the vowel sound. What's the word? What's the word?'.

Walking towards her was her colleague; a square-jawed woman, who marched relentlessly and unsmilingly along the corridors. She dragged her resentment and her Special Needs students with her.

Lisa Jenner, the supply teacher who had been hit in the face by a can at Westgate College, was not enjoying her week's placement at the academy. In fact she was praying inwardly for the immediate return of the sickly teacher whose class she was teaching. At lunchtime, after escaping the oppressive atmosphere of the staff room, she had tried to retreat to her car for five minutes. She found that her little metal haven of calm had been locked into the school car park and she would not be able to gain access to it until home time at three o'clock.

Supply Line agency had used some of the teaching staff here as models for the robots that they were trialling in the other XLSys schools. They have had a little difficulty with the Helper 9000 (Phonics model) of late. It keeps getting stuck with the stock phrase "Read the word, repeat the vowel sound. Read the word, read the word, read, read, r,r,r,r,r, read…."

Emptying out his book bag that evening little Connor Chapman, from Year Three, enjoys his after-school drink and a biscuit. He wants to tell his mum something, really badly.
'Mum, mum, my teacher is a robot, and so are all the other teachers.'
Jackie Chapman laughed. 'Connor, I am really glad you've got a good imagination, but you must know that's not true…Are you reading a book about robots at the moment?'
'Mum, I'm not lying, she *really* is a robot'.
That evening, when Jackie Chapman's husband, Adrian, arrived home from a long day in London, she said
'Connor says his teacher's a robot, what do you think I should do about it?'.
'I don't know about his class teacher, but the headteacher is pretty scary.' Adrian added.
Adrian had really hated school himself and just being back at school, even for half an hour or so, gave him a sick feeling in his stomach.

6.

At Westgate College it is now January, certain teachers are not going to be returning to the school. Their jobs have been *rationalised;* they are sitting at home staring out of their kitchen windows at their cold and waterlogged gardens.

Mr. Hughes, from Physics, and Ms. Smith, from Modern Foreign Languages, are missing their students; who kept them by turns challenged and entertained. The students, for their part, are also missing them. Mr. Hughes and Ms. Smith both provided their students with knowledge which would both prepare them for life outside school and also help them pass those all-important exams. These teachers didn't want to leave, but in the end they felt that they really didn't have any choice.

The new teachers have taken their place, they are efficient and relentless; they will get you your grade 9*, but they won't be people you will want to bump into later in life. You would cross the street or take the next train to get away from these grey, humourless automatons.

At break times some of the new staff patrol the corridors. They are wearing fluorescent jackets and carrying walkie-talkies. Their habit of wearing sunglasses indoors would make it easy to imagine that they are not human.

XLSys Academy Trust
To all Staff: Targets in Teaching

In life there are winners and losers, the same is true of your classroom. There are students who are ready to fly and students who will never achieve anything in life. At XLSys we believe in a no-nonsense approach to teaching. Therefore we recommend that all staff target their teaching at the top 25% of students.

*Ofteach are **not** interested in grades 4 and below. Therefore from now on please grade all your students accordingly. Grades 4 and below students will be taught in the hall by the cover staff and teaching assistants. This targeted teaching method will be sure to guarantee the school an "Outstanding" grade from Ofteach.*

*N.B. Staff are reminded that failure to follow this regime will be regarded as a **deliberate transgression** of the contract signed with XLSys at the beginning of the school year.*

Jean-Marie Cadeux and Ellie-Mae Brown are not going to achieve even so much as a Grade 3, Grade 4 would be beyond their wildest dreams. Jean-Marie came to England when he was ten. He dreams of being a rapper, but first of all he must analyse Macbeth and quote phrases from "A Christmas Carol". Ellie-Mae has a very poor attendance record and the kind of home life that the XLSys Academy Trust does not want to know about.

During Maths, English and Science lessons they are often herded into the assembly hall to watch a film or play board games. They are watched over by the supply teachers and the teaching assistants; who are every bit as bored and resentful as the students. Even though behaviour was sometimes poor in the good old days, at least the children felt valued for their individuality. Now they are made to feel like one great anonymous herd: the under-achievers, the unwanted and the under-valued.

Jean-Marie and Ellie-Mae are definitely mourning the good old days of WC. They saw Mr. Hughes, the Physics teacher, in the town centre the other day. He looked like he had lost the will to live; they took turns to sneak a look at him. It was like seeing a wounded soldier. Maybe if he saw the children staring at him he might lose the remaining dignity that he had left? Ellie-Mae has had an idea; she doesn't think she is going to pass any of her exams so what has she got to lose?
'Jean, I dare you to throw something at that teacher's head....do it for Mr. Hughes' sake!'.

Jean-Marie is on the same trajectory, there is no way he is going to get good grades. He and Ellie-Mae will be in the assembly hall until the exams start, so what the hell!

The can soars through the air and hits the selected target on the temple. The supply teacher is a woman, probably about fifty; she calls herself Mrs. McDonald. As the can hits her temple there is a strangely metallic clank; not what anyone was expecting. Her eyes close for a moment and then all havoc breaks loose.

Within a second of the can hitting its target the teacher's chin suddenly pulls smartly inwards and her eyes close shut. As her head points towards the floor, there is a whirring sound and then she raises her head smartly and her eyes snap open. "Mrs. McDonald" is a variant of the MK5000 model. Its speciality is sarcasm and belittling of children. Suddenly, and alarmingly the robot starts spouting off, in machine-gun fashion, its full inventory of belittlement.

'What do you call that? Is it a diagram? I thought a three year old had drawn it…..Are you talking or are you just taking up valuable oxygen from cleverer students?…..Have you had your hair cut this weekend or did you lie down in front of the lawnmower? No, you can't go to the toilet, let's wait until there's a puddle on the floor. I know you are from the Special Needs department, but there's no need to make it so obvious.'

As she reached the end of each phrase of insults the robotic teacher would then power down for a second and then instantly restart.

After the third complete round of insults had temporarily ceased, the students looked at each other. Then in silent agreement all of them removed their phones from their pockets and started filming the remarkable events. By the end of the lesson Mytube was receiving the film and lessons across Westgate were being disrupted; as students across the town tuned in to view it.

It was the subject of the regional news report that very evening. Mr. Murray was on a damage-limitation exercise; he thought a little creative storytelling might do the trick.

The seasoned news anchor, Jenny Tomlinson, who Mr. Murray had always had a crush on, pulled no punches in her interview.
'Mr. Murray, some parents will feel that you do not care about their children and you are just fobbing them off with unqualified staff,' she said, looking at Mr. Murray in a most unfriendly manner.
'Well, Jenny, as I've said before all XLSys Academy schools are completely committed to all of our students. This is just an example of childish mischievousness and, in any case, it was all filmed with the co-operation of the Drama department.'
Mr. Murray smiled broadly at the camera, in what he hoped was a friendly smile; it was not, it was as convincing as a smile from Caligula.
'Mr. Murray isn't it true that your Trust have abolished Drama from the curriculum? So I am rather at a loss to understand your explanation.'
But Mr. Murray just went on smiling his hideous smile at the camera. After all Jenny Tomlinson may well be an attractive news presenter of a certain age, but she had still missed one crucial point: most of the academy's students were now being taught by robots.

7.

Some of the parents were not so impressed, especially those whose children had been spending most of their lessons in the assembly hall. So on

Monday morning Mr. Murray still had an angry inbox of emails; which he forwarded to his secretary for her to deal with. Keith Murray is not so easily dissuaded or distracted; he wants to crack on with the next phase of the improvement programme, Phase 9.

The exams are fast approaching; this will be his time to shine. Exam results make or break a school, Mr. Murray is only too aware of that. In the large draughty sports hall a variant of the HELPER9000 is being used to read and scribe for the exams.
The students file in and are eventually all seated. Now is the time they have all been waiting for, no turning back now.

The exams go as clockwork; this is where robot teaching assistants really come into their own. Everything was done correctly and to the letter. The reading of the questions was all done at exactly the correct monotone level and the scribing was accurate and legible. At the end of the exams all of the HELPER9000s were simply powered down and put in the exam cupboard until next time. I just hope somebody took the batteries out.

Come the third week of August and the local news team were parked outside Westgate College waiting for the students to come and collect their results in person. Mr. Murray has been at the school since early this morning. He knows exactly who he expects to have done well in their exams and he will be delighted to have his picture in the local press; as the school takes the credit for all their pupils' hard work.

Holding their GCSE certificates in front of them, the head boy and the head girl of the school are interviewed by the local news team. Kaylee Evans has passed eleven GCSEs, all with starred grade 9s. She smiles dazzlingly at the camera.
'I couldn't have passed my exams without going to an XLSys Academy school,' she says.

Keith Murray looks on like a proud parent; Phase 9 has been a success. As he powers down the Kaylee Mk1 model that evening and returns it to the stock cupboard, he sends a voice memo to himself.
'Note to self, Phase 9 successful. Phase 10 order ten more Kaylees and put in an order for a prototype Kyle Mk 1 Head Boy model.'

This is a work of fiction. Names, characters, businesses, places, events, locales, and incidents are either the products of the author's imagination or used in a fictitious manner. Any resemblance to actual persons, living or dead, or actual events is purely coincidental.

Find out more about the author:

Lizzie's website:
lizziejarrett.co.uk
lizziejarrett.com
Twitter: LizzieJarrettUnreal @LizzieJarrett9
Facebook: Lizzie Jarrett (writer page)